Best Wishes

Val P. (Voinks)

Voinks submitted her first short story to a women's magazine at the tender age of nine. Although the response was a kind rejection letter, she didn't give up on her literary ambitions. She carried on writing novels, short stories, poetry, songs and even theatre scripts for friends and family.

Many years later an accident caused her to be housebound for two years. This gave her the perfect opportunity to dedicate time to completing her first published manuscript. Chance remarks from visitors, strangers and even life itself continue to supply inspiration for future works.

She lives in a South London suburb, and her nickname came about from... Ah, but that's another story!

Changes

Ch-Ch changes

VOINKS

Changes

Ch-Ch changes

Olympia Publishers
London

www.olympiapublishers.com
OLYMPIA PAPERBACK EDITION

Copyright © Voinks 2013

The right of Voinks to be identified as author of
this work has been asserted in accordance with sections 77 and 78 of the
Copyright, Designs and Patents Act 1988.

All Rights Reserved

No reproduction, copy or transmission of this publication
may be made without written permission.
No paragraph of this publication may be reproduced,
copied or transmitted save with the written permission of the publisher, or in
accordance with the provisions
of the Copyright Act 1956 (as amended).

Any person who commits any unauthorised act in relation to
this publication may be liable to criminal
prosecution and civil claims for damage.

A CIP catalogue record for this title is
available from the British Library.

ISBN: 978-1-84897-299-5

(Olympia Publishers is part of Ashwell Publishing Ltd)

This is a work of fiction.
Names, characters, places and incidents originate from the writer's
imagination. Any resemblance to actual persons, living or dead, is purely
coincidental.

First Published in 2013

Olympia Publishers
60 Cannon Street
London
EC4N 6NP

Printed in Great Britain

Dedication

To everyone who reads books,
and the authors who write them!

Contents

CHAPTER 1 — 15
THE BEGINNING OF THE CHANGE

CHAPTER 2 — 21
THE NEXT DAY

CHAPTER 3 — 23
MOVING ON

CHAPTER 4 — 30
LIVING THE LIFE

CHAPTER 5 — 32
SETTLING IN

CHAPTER 6 — 36
WAS THERE EVER ANOTHER LIFE?

CHAPTER 7 — 39
NEW FRIENDS

CHAPTER 8 — 42
THE MORNING AFTER

CHAPTER 9 — 45
MORE GOODBYES

CHAPTER 10 — 52
A NORMAL DAY

CHAPTER 11 — 54
RED FACED AND SUNBURNT

CHAPTER 12   61
     ALONE BUT NOT LONELY

CHAPTER 13   62
     A DAY OF CONTRASTS

CHAPTER 14   70
     WHAT NOW? WHAT NEXT? WHERE TO?

CHAPTER 15   76
     LEGALESE AND MORE DEVELOPMENTS

CHAPTER 16   82
     DECISIONS

CHAPTER 17   87
     MOVING ON

CHAPTER 18   90
     A NEW BEGINNING

CHAPTER 19   95
     LIFE MOVES ON

CHAPTER 20   101
     PRACTICALITIES AND SURPRISES

CHAPTER 21   112
     A PERFECT DAY

CHAPTER 22   120
     SETTING A ROUTINE

CHAPTER 23   128
     THE MORNING AFTER

CHAPTER 24   132
     REVELATIONS

CHAPTER 25 PREPARATIONS	**137**
CHAPTER 26 EXPLORING	**140**
CHAPTER 27 PLANS AND PRACTICALITIES	**142**
CHAPTER 28 REUNIONS AND REVELATIONS	**146**
CHAPTER 29 MEETING THE FAMILY	**152**
CHAPTER 30 DREAMS AND REALITIES	**160**
CHAPTER 31 PLANS AND ORGANISATION	**166**
CHAPTER 32 MORE ORGANISATION	**167**
CHAPTER 33 PREPARATIONS	**168**
CHAPTER 34 PEOPLE AND PARTIES	**172**
CHAPTER 35 A DAY OF SURPRISES	**176**
CHAPTER 36 BACK TO THE AIRPORT	**181**
CHAPTER 37 LONDON	**183**
CHAPTER 38 THE END AND THE BEGINNING	**189**

Chapter 1
The beginning of the change

Jane slowly opened her eyes, and lay thinking about the events of the last three months.

She still couldn't believe that after sharing the house and spending all their time together since the death of their parents, ten years ago, her older sister Jena had met, fallen in love and married a man she had only known for a few months.

Glancing at the bedside clock, she realised that Jena and Mark would now be well on their way to starting their new life together in Australia.

Soon they would be greeting the warm sunshine, not looking out at another cold, grey, drizzly, London morning.

Used to her set routine of getting up and driving the few miles to her job in the small family run business where she had worked for over fifteen years, Jane felt somewhat at a loss with the empty day stretching before her.

She had known for some time that old man Baker had been wanting to retire, pass the business onto his sons and move to his retirement home in Spain for the sake of his arthritis.

Even though she hadn't the same respect for the boys that she had for the old man, she didn't expect that they would sell the business within a month of his retirement and give all the staff one month's notice.

She had just assumed that they would carry on as before and that although they might make some small changes, selling out to a whiz-kid, go-getting, American company hadn't even been a consideration.

The new company had gone through the motions of giving her an interview but both she and they knew that the 'profit at all costs' mentality was not for her.

Perhaps she had become complacent and out of touch but Mr Baker senior had still managed to make a decent living whilst retaining old world courtesy to customers. She agreed that was the way business should be done.

They say everything comes in threes and her win on the lottery was at least one good thing to come out of the last few months. She still had to pinch herself when she realised that the money sitting in the bank, together with her redundancy pay, carefully invested, was enough to let her have a reasonable living without ever having to work again.

The thought actually filled her with dread. She enjoyed the routine of nine to five, using her brain in problem solving and the satisfaction of a job well done.

Now, with nothing to structure her life and not even having her sister to talk things over with, the empty days seemed to stretch endlessly in front of her.

Mentally shaking herself, she got out of bed, bathed, dressed, ate breakfast and realised it was still only 8.30. Everything was packed and ready for the storage company to collect on Friday, ready for the new owners of the house to move in at the end of the month.

Although she had half-heartedly looked at some flats to buy, now that the house was too big for her on her own, she hadn't found anything that felt right.

Rather than rush into a purchase that she might later regret, she had taken the decision to put her belongings into storage for a while and move, temporarily, into a small local hotel while she sorted out what she wanted to do.

Glancing at the clock again, she saw that forty minutes had passed and she had done nothing except daydream and waste time.

Needing to do something, Jane grabbed her coat, keys and handbag and before she knew it she was in the High Street gazing, without seeing, into the windows of shops that were just waking up for the new day.

Even her favourite junk shop, which pretentiously called itself Antiques4U, couldn't motivate her. What was the point of buying more things when she soon wouldn't even have a house to put them in?

Wandering aimlessly, and with time to kill, she turned up a side street she didn't often use and found herself staring at the window of a shop with a 'Grand Opening' banner blazed across its windows.

Intrigued she saw that it boasted 'Complete makeovers for the modern woman' and wondered what such a shop, which rightly belonged in the West End, was doing opening up in her local suburban town.

Before she could ponder further on how long they might stay in business, the door was flung open and she was gushed at by a woman nearing 40, probably only a few years older than her, although the contrast couldn't have been more marked.

Whereas her own mousy brown hair hung down to her shoulders in a style best described as 'au naturel', even at this time of the morning the shop owner looked as if she had just stepped out of the hairdresser's, was wearing full makeup, jewellery and what looked like a designer dress.

Before she could protest she had been ushered inside, draped in a silk gown and seated in front of a full-length mirror, being examined as if she was some sort of specimen.

Three hours later she felt as if she was looking at a model in a magazine. She couldn't believe the thirty-something, sophisticated lady with short, cropped, blonde hair, dazzling blue eyes and subtle makeup, was actually her.

Although she did a double take at the size of the bill, she realised with a sense of wonder that it actually wouldn't even make a dent in her now sizeable savings.

Feeling surreal, she walked back to the main shopping area and realised she was hungry. She fleetingly thought of going home to make a sandwich, or to having something at the local café, but instead found herself outside the best hotel in the area, looking at the discreet sign advertising à la carte lunch from 12 until 3.

Although she had never actually been there before, she knew from colleagues that it was the sort of place you went for posh wedding receptions, Golden Wedding anniversaries, or similar occasions when you really wanted to push the boat out.

Suddenly she was shocked out of her reverie by a resounding wolf whistle. Turning to see who had been whistled at, she realised she was the object of attention from a young, fit, guy in a builder's van.

Not sure whether to be pleased or embarrassed, before she knew it she had walked into the hotel to be greeted by the maîtres d' and seated at a table, with a large menu in her hands.

Ordering the tuna Milanese with Chef's special vegetables comfit, it didn't seem right to ask for orange juice so she opted for the half bottle of Macon Latour that the sommelier had recommended. After an excellent meal and coffee and feeling more relaxed than she had for a long while, she glanced round at the other occupants of the pristine dining room. There were a few small tables with ladies that lunch but mainly the room was filled with men in suits, obviously conducting important business meetings with large contracts up for grabs.

Surprisingly she didn't feel out of place – she still had the feeling that shortly she would wake up and return to being the staid spinster who had been overtaken by the events in her life.

Still in somewhat of a dream, she paid her bill and again found herself looking in a shop window. This time her attention had been caught by a display for cruises to the sun, with people sipping cocktails by the pool-side bar and laughing happily, knowing they were the elite and all was right with the world.

When a middle-aged man held the door open for her as he was coming out, she had no choice but to go into the travel agents and was immediately greeted by a young man with a big smile for his prospective customer.

Although confused at first by her lack of idea as to actually what she wanted, fifty minutes later she emerged clutching a folder with her itinerary for a Mediterranean island, five star hotel, flight, and full travel arrangements. Booked and paid for on her credit card.

For a moment her practical brain wondered if she had been imagining how much the salesman had been flirting with her just to achieve his sale.

Then, catching a glimpse of herself in the window on the way out, she was stunned by the reflection she saw and realised that perhaps beautiful women get more perks than dowdy old maids.

As she was passing the local train station she noticed that the next train to London was due in three minutes and on an impulse she bought a ticket. Thirty minutes later she was in the West End.

Despite the dreary weather, Oxford Street was bustling with tourists and again without really thinking about it, she found herself in an exclusive boutique being fawned over.

Later she thought she had just intended to get out of the rain, but having spent more than a month's salary in one day and throwing caution to the wind, she tore up her return train ticket and hailed a taxi to take her home.

Looking through her purchases and unable to resist patting her newly cropped hair, she stared in disbelief at her holiday ticket. She who was always so organised had even left the ticket open-ended for the return journey, which was so totally out of character she still felt as if she would wake up at any minute and find it was still 7 o'clock on Monday morning, and the day had been a dream.

Returning to her more practical self, she opened up her computer and looked up details on how to actually check in at the airport, luggage restrictions and what she should be aware of when travelling abroad.

With a start she realised she wasn't even sure if her passport was up to date.

Apart from school trips and the odd group organised shopping trip to France, her holidays had usually been either spent at home, decorating and relaxing, or coach trips with her sister exploring the delights of the English countryside.

Feeling she had actually woken up she reverted to her usual efficient self. She found her expired passport, completed documentation for renewal, and set about organising the minute details which usually dominated her life, making To-Do lists and ticking off the smallest details as they were completed, so that everything ran smoothly.

With a start she realised that it was gone midnight. What a strange day. She felt as if she was two different people in one body: the dowdy, middle-aged, mousy, efficient, woman and the sophisticated blonde who caused men to look twice, or took off for the continent at the drop of a hat.

Time for bed. Tomorrow is another day.

Chapter 2
The next day

Jane woke as usual at 7 and lay there for a moment letting her mind wander. Through the curtains she could see the sun trying to come out. It looked as if it was going to be a nice day.

Her thoughts drifted back to the day before and, still half asleep, she tried to get her brain functioning to sort out whether she had dreamed everything, or if it had actually happened.

She subconsciously put her hand up to her hair and realising that her brown tatty locks were now designer blonde, she realised it was all true.

Feeling motivated, she jumped out of bed and focused on organising her wardrobe, found her suitcase and started making her usual lists:

Face cream, mobile, mobile charger, body cream, toothbrush, toothpaste, need to organise currency, increase her credit card limit, do bank transfers from her savings account to cover her expenditure.

Butterflies fluttered in her stomach but for the first time in ages, she actually felt alive, felt she had a purpose to her life again.

Down to the Post Office to sort out her passport, noticing the admiring glances from men passing by. Initially she thought they were looking at someone else but gradually she began to accept this is Jane, the head turner, not Jane the mouse that no one notices.

Stopping at the chemist, she browsed the extensive range of suntan creams and lotions, trying to work out whether a factor ten was better than a factor five.

Did she tan easily? She hadn't a clue! Sun protection was not something she had needed before in England, even at the height of summer.

Taking advice from the assistant, she was astounded to realise that she had spent nearly £50 on the various tubes and sprays now weighing down her carrier bag.

With the plastic digging into her hands, her attention was caught by a large designer tote beach bag in a boutique window.

'In for a penny, in for a pound' she thought as she entered the shop to buy the bag. Before she left she was also the proud owner of three bikinis – two of them so minute she couldn't see herself ever wearing them.

A final stop at the bank to order some euros, sort out her savings and she was ready for home and something to eat.

She spent the afternoon browsing through her purchases of the last two days and wondered what on earth had got into her lately.

Logging on to her laptop she found an e-mail from Jena, full of news of her new home, and how fantastic everything was.

Jane couldn't help wondering how her sister could have so much news when she had been away less than forty-eight hours, then realised how much she herself had changed in the same time period.

Almost for the sake of something to say, she replied briefly to Jena that she had decided to take a short holiday, so not to worry if she didn't hear from her for a while.

The next morning was again bright and sunny with a gentle breeze. She enjoyed the fresh air as she walked to keep her 11 o'clock appointment with the solicitors to sort out the final paperwork for the sale of the house.

Then a call into the offices of the storage company. Everything was under control, the lorry would be with her between 10 and 11 the next morning.

Chapter 3
Moving on

Jane made one final check of her flight bag. Passport, credit card, currency, booking confirmation, mobile, laptop, book, purse and wallet. All present and correct.

She was still a bit apprehensive that she didn't actually have a ticket for the flight.

It seemed strange that her passport and a piece of paper showing the flight details, printed by a computer, were all she needed to be able to board the plane.

A beep from outside, followed by a call on her mobile, confirmed the cab was waiting.

She collected her suitcases and took a final glance round at her childhood home. Funny to think this would be the last time she would see it.

Taking a deep breath, she doubled locked the door and put the spare keys through the letterbox for the new owners to find when they moved in the next morning.

For a moment she was surprised how eagerly the cab driver rushed to help her, taking her suitcases to stow in the boot and making sure she was comfortable.

Then she realised that she was actually getting used to this type of attention and even enjoying it. After a final glance back at the house, she settled down to enjoy the trip to the airport.

With the cab driver flirting outrageously with her, the time soon passed and before she knew it they were pulling into the departure's drop-off point.

After paying off the cab, she stood for a moment, slightly unsure what to do next.

Her dilemma was soon solved by a porter rushing up, loading her cases onto a trolley and leading her efficiently to the appropriate check-in desk.

Having been persuaded by the travel agent to fly first class, she only had to wait for two businessmen to be processed before she was being asked for her passport and issued with her boarding pass.

She didn't even have to lift her cases onto the weighing machine, one of the two businessmen having stayed behind to carry out this small service for her.

With a smile and a word of thanks, she carefully put her documentation into her travel wallet and hoisting her bag onto her shoulder, set off towards the security check.

Being somewhat of a green traveller, she had looked up on the Internet exactly what she had to do. Before she knew it she had passed through the security arch and was in the departure lounge, gazing round at all the shops lining the walls.

With plenty of time to kill, she spent nearly an hour window-shopping then, after a quick coffee and pastry, she saw that it was only a few minutes before her flight would be called.

She took out her boarding pass for one final check, then a glance at the flight display told her it was now time to make her way to Gate 15.

She had already worked out where she would have to go and after again producing her passport and boarding card, was soon seated in the departure gate.

Glancing round, she saw that she was one of the first to arrive, but shortly afterwards the area began to fill up rapidly. There seemed to be only one or two families.

Although there were a couple of groups of youngsters, in jeans and T-shirts, chatting and laughing excitedly, in the main the other passengers seemed to be elderly couples or businessmen, either singly or in pairs, working on their laptops.

In no time at all she was being led along a short passage and with a start, found that she was actually inside the plane and being shown to her seat.

She felt as if she was the only one listening to the stewardess explaining about seat belts and safety procedures and thought everyone else must have heard it hundreds of times before.

Safely buckled in and with her hand luggage stowed away, she felt the butterflies in her stomach as the engine roared and her hands tightly gripped the armrests.

Then, suddenly, the exhilaration took over, her grip loosened, and she found herself with a big grin on her face enjoying the rush.

She had to bite her lip to stop herself yelling with joy as the tyres left the ground and they were swooping higher and higher into the clouds, banking into a turn and then settling into a steady flight with the drone of the engines as a background.

Too excited to read, she just looked out of the window, watching the houses getting smaller and smaller and the scenery slowly changing until her view was obscured by the plane going through thick white clouds.

She felt as if she was riding through candyfloss and smiled to herself when she realised that despite the sophisticated exterior, inside was a giggly, excited, child.

Her reverie was interrupted by the stewardess offering her a pre-dinner drink and rather than opt for her usual plain orange juice, she decided to lace it up with a large vodka.

For the first time she looked round at her fellow passengers and realised that the businessman who had helped her with her suitcases at check-in was smiling at her from across the aisle, trying to catch her attention.

Returning his smile but feeling rather embarrassed, she turned her head back to look out of the window again.

The clouds had cleared and now she could see snow-capped mountains in the distance.

She was fascinated by the peaks and crags and the way the setting sun was bouncing off the mountain slopes, emphasising the white glare of the snow and ice.

Her attention was diverted by the stewardess handing her a meal tray and asking her what was her wine preference. While she was dithering, the hostess suggested perhaps a half bottle of the Chablis would be a good choice to go with the speciality chicken dish, which was the main course. A creamy fish mousse starter, and a pastry concoction with fruit and nuts left her feeling comfortably replete. After all the unaccustomed alcohol she was glad of the coffee to help ward off the feeling of sleepiness which had started to overtake her.

The announcement that they would shortly be coming in to land made her brain snap back into gear. Looking out of the window yet again, she could see in the gathering darkness the outline of a rocky island surrounded by the dark waters of what she assumed must be the Mediterranean Sea.

Gradually the shape of various buildings moulded themselves into towns and villages, with their twinkling lights battling the forthcoming darkness.

The increasing roar of the engines made her realise that they had landed and were now taxiing gently to their parking spot, with the lights of the terminal sparkling close by.

Collecting her belongings she was ushered with the other passengers to the bus which deposited them at the entrance to the air terminal.

Alighting from the bus, she turned on hearing a voice saying "Hello," to find her businessman from the plane once again smiling at her.

After introducing himself as Greg Masters and asking her name, she found herself walking in step with him towards passport control.

Having cleared immigration without problem, he then escorted her to the luggage reclaim, where he helped her retrieve her suitcases, loaded them on a trolley and pushed them for her through customs.

He seemed very disappointed when she declined his offer of a lift to her hotel as she had noticed a chauffeur holding a board with her name on it, arranged by the travel agents.

Before she left he thrust his business card into her hand and pleaded with her to call him so he could take her out for dinner one evening.

After identifying herself to the waiting driver, her bags were efficiently loaded into the luxurious car and soon she was speeding away from the airport, along darkened streets with unfamiliar buildings.

All her senses felt alert as she took in the different sounds and smells of a country so different from her London home.

For a moment she felt quite emotional as she realised that she was in effect homeless but she pulled herself together as they pulled up in front of a beautiful building which looked like a castle. Bougainvillaea cascaded over the ancient thick, pale, stone walls, their scent drifting on the slight evening breeze and although the sun had long gone down, the air still felt pleasantly warm.

Despite the meal on the plane, the appetising smell of food cooking made her realise that she was actually quite hungry. A few weeks of this she thought to herself, and I'll have put on so much weight I'll need two seats to myself for the flight back.

With a start she realised that she was enjoying herself, and not looking forward to returning to a grey and dismal London.

A few minutes later she had successfully checked in and was sitting on the bed of a beautiful en-suite room with her luggage on the floor besides her.

Getting up, she crossed to the old-fashioned lead glassed window and flinging it wide open, was greeted by the sight of landscaped flower gardens, leading down to a private beach and beyond that the gentle rolling sea.

Even from here she could hear the whisper of waves undulating softly onto the beach and smell the slightly salty scent, mixed with seaweed and other pleasant aromas that she could not identify.

Returning to sit on the bed, she found a glossy brochure outlining all the amenities of the hotel and the local area. Although the times of breakfast, lunch and dinner were all wide ranging, there was also a 24-hour room service.

Despite having two outdoor and one indoor swimming pools, a Jacuzzi and a steam room, there was also a regular courtesy taxi to the beach, a beauty shop, various bars and lounges, and organised trips upon request. In fact everything she could think of to make her stay as enjoyable as possible.

Pulling herself together she moved from the window, leaving it open and crossed to her waiting suitcases. There was plenty of room for all her clothes in the heavy oak, antique, wardrobe which although slightly old fashioned, was beautifully carved and suited the ambience of the Castille Hotel perfectly.

The matching chest of drawers took all her underwear and with her passport and other valuables safely stowed in the safe she had found built into the wardrobe, she crossed to the connecting door which she assumed was the bathroom.

Although still in keeping with the old-world charm of the place, the modern bathroom housed not only a deep, luxurious bath, but also a shower, two immense washbasins, a hairdryer, bidet and heated towel rails, complete with pristine white fluffy towels.

Glancing in the large ornate mirror, she was still taken aback by the blonde, sophisticated lady that was her reflection. Feeling decidedly grubby after the long day spent travelling, she decided to take advantage of the bath with a good long soak.

Emerging forty minutes later with her hair and skin feeling fresh and delicately perfumed, courtesy of the small bottles thoughtfully provided by the hotel, she crossed back to the wardrobe to select what she should wear for the evening.

A shoe-string strapped, long, V-necked cotton evening dress, one of her impulse buys, caught her attention. Slipping it on, she again gazed in wonder at the vision looking back at her, so different from the staid spinster she had been only a few short weeks ago.

After applying some light makeup and selecting a discreet necklace and earrings she felt ready to face the world, full of confidence.

It was only as she locked the door behind her that she felt some momentary qualms. Here she was, an inexperienced traveller, alone in a foreign country, in a strange hotel, with no friends or family even aware of where she was staying. She was totally on her own with no one to call upon if disaster struck.

Taking a deep breath, she lifted her chin, stretched herself to her full height and set off down the corridor in search of the dining room.

Chapter 4
Living the life

Jane woke to the feel of a warm sun on her face and the smell of the sea.

Slightly to her surprise, she was immediately aware of where she was and what she was doing there.

Stretching luxuriously in the comfortable king size bed, she let her mind rewind to when she had left her room to go to dinner the previous night.

Easily finding the reception area, she was shown to the outside dining room and escorted to a small table under a partially covered awning on the roof.

Surrounded by potted plants in full bloom, with the majority of the area open to the fresh evening air and a small band playing soft music in the background, she felt totally content to sit and watch the world go by.

The tables were set just far enough apart to ensure privacy but close enough not to feel left out. The service was perfect, attentive to her every need, but not intrusive.

Despite having eaten on the plane, she found herself spoilt for choice from the extensive menu and despite skipping a starter, still managed to enjoy a full main course, followed by a light but delicious airy dessert, and another half bottle of wine.

What else could she do but accept the offer of a complimentary local liquor to go with her coffee. It would have been churlish to refuse. At least that was what she was trying to convince herself.

As the evening progressed and the wine flowed, the music changed from subtle background to more upbeat. She was surprised but pleased when a man about five or six years her junior, held out his hand to her and even more surprised with herself when she accepted his offer to dance, returning to her table a while later, feeling flushed but happy.

Although the exercise had been welcomed after all the sitting around and eating she had done that day, she knew that in reality she had been feeling slightly lonely. The easy-going companionship and light-hearted flattery of the young man and his friends had made her feel good.

The elderly gentleman at the next table smiled at her as she sat down, puffing slightly from the exertions of the disco type beat and complimented her on her dancing.

Even though he was obviously in his seventies, she couldn't help smiling at the way he was openly flirting with her, even when his wife jokingly admonished him that a beautiful young girl like that wouldn't be interested in an old fogey like him.

It was a long time since she had been called a girl, even if he was nearly old enough to be her grandfather, or at least her father.

She felt herself envying their obviously close, loving, relationship and after they had got up for the anniversary waltz, was not surprised to hear that they were celebrating their 50th wedding anniversary on the island where he had been stationed during his wartime service.

Despite Martha's protests, she was happy to be regaled with photos of their children and grandchildren and to hear the pride when Bert told her all about the one who was a doctor, the teacher and the one studying to be a lawyer, even the granddaughter who was at university despite the sadness of her parents' divorce.

When both Bert and Martha kissed her cheek to say goodnight, she felt as if she had known and loved them all her life.

She was surprised to see that it was already 11.30 and the evening had flown by without her even noticing.

Chapter 5
Settling in

With a fond smile on her face, from the happy memories of the previous evening, Jane got up and selected a light summer dress ready to face the day ahead.

She thought she would start by exploring the local area and getting to know something of the culture and history of the island which was to be her home for the next few weeks.

Armed with the information she had downloaded from the Internet before she left, her tote bag containing some of the sun creams she had purchased, some currency and her keys she set off.

Stopping at reception, she picked up a few tourist flyers of places of local interest and was advised that the next courtesy bus would be leaving from outside the hotel in a few minutes, dropping off at the local town.

Leaning back in her seat, she relaxed in the air-conditioned twelve-seater bus, enjoying the sunshine streaming through the windows. Her fellow trippers were mainly elderly couples and she wasn't sure if she was pleased or disappointed to find that Martha and Bert were not amongst them,

Some ten minutes later she found herself in a pretty village square with her mind buzzing about the times and pick up places for the return journey, if she wanted to take advantage of them.

Unsure of her plans, she thought to herself that rather than be time bound and restricted, she could always get a taxi back to the hotel, after all she could afford it.

With the sun on her face and the day before her, she wandered up the small, narrow, side streets, discovering tiny hidden shops in the most unlikely places, always being welcomed with a smile, whether she bought something or not.

Most of the shopkeepers just seemed pleased to have a new face to chat to in their broken, but understandable, English and she soon got used to being asked what in London would be intrusive questions.

'How many children did she have, why wasn't she married to a nice man, was she rich, what did she do for a living?' Surprisingly she wasn't upset by the questions.

Instead, she even found she was asking herself why she wasn't married with 2.4 children, living in a semi with access to good local schools, with a husband who caught the 5.15 from London and expected his dinner on the table at 6.30 every evening.

Perhaps she should have been taking the children to football and ballet lessons, making love on Saturdays and anniversaries, and taking a fortnight's holiday once a year, maybe to a cottage in Devon where she would still do housework and cook a meal, just on a strange oven.

'Therein lies the answer?' she thought.

Instead she was even learning a few words of the local language, a strange mixture of Italian and Arabic with a bit of English thrown in for good luck and loving every minute of it.

Somehow it didn't matter that it wasn't a knight in shining armour who was teaching her, but a wizened old man or woman, with a toothless smile, a brown face and dark, antique, clothing. They wanted to know everything about her and were proud of their ability to speak English, even if some of the things they said made her smile at their twisted interpretation.

Thinking about it, what they said made perfect sense. 'Did you come by car, come by bus, or come by walk?' She was almost tempted to lie and say she came by walk, just because it was such a lovely expression.

Almost reluctantly she had to bid her new friends goodbye, otherwise she would have spent all day in small, gloomy shops.

Promising to visit them again soon, she retraced her steps to the modern, bustling, tourist areas with shops whose names she recognised, although the ancient buildings they were housed in looked so different from the modern brickwork of her home town.

Finding a modern Italian style glass and steel building, she settled down at an outside table to have lunch, watch the passers-by, browse her tourist guides and decide how she would spend her afternoon.

For such a small island she was surprised at how much history it held. She made a mental note that the next day she would investigate the various archaeological sites which abounded in the area.

For now, the sun was too welcoming and after paying for her lunch, she found herself drawn to the local harbour.

Despite living in town, she had always loved the sea and finding a bench near the shore, she sat down to watch the fishermen bringing in their catch, mending their nets, and repairing their boats.

Before she knew it the sun was going down, and shaking herself out of her lethargy, she made her way back to the meeting point to catch the 6.15 bus back to the hotel.

Catching sight of herself in the mirror prior to her bath, she was surprised to see that her skin had taken on a healthy ruddy-brown glow. Without even trying she had the makings of a suntan.

So much for all the expensive creams and potions she had bought, which were still in their packaging.

Making her way down to reception and not sure that she wanted to stay confined in the hotel for another evening meal, she heard her name called and was handed the phone by reception.

Somehow Greg had found out where she was staying and had called to ask if she was free to have dinner with him that night. Caught on the hop she agreed and fifteen minutes later, he walked into the hotel foyer, planted a kiss on her cheek and guided her to the waiting taxi.

She found herself in the more exclusive part of town at what was obviously an expensive restaurant. Greg was the perfect dinner companion, explaining how he had noticed the name tag on her luggage and phoned round all the likely hotels until he had found out where she was registered.

He seemed genuinely pleased that he had managed to catch her in time to take her out to dinner, assuming that she would have a full itinerary and be unable to spare the time to meet up with him during his short business trip.

She learnt that he was divorced, no children and an advisor for a merchant bank specialising in offshore investments and living in Hertfordshire.

Unsure how much to divulge of her own life, she merely said that she had recently sold her home and was taking a short break before deciding where she would start house hunting.

He seemed to accept that the funding for the expensive hotel came from the sale of the house, so she didn't have to explain about her lottery win, or how her life was in limbo at the moment.

When they had finished their meal and ordered coffee and liquors he asked her to dance. Although she had enjoyed his company, she felt herself withdrawing when he started kissing and caressing her neck. He was good looking, charming, and made her feel good, but she didn't want to be another notch on the bedpost, and to be honest, he wasn't really her type.

When he eventually dropped her back at her hotel at around 1 a.m. it wasn't difficult for her to gently but firmly make the decision that he couldn't come back to her room for a nightcap.

Instead she thanked him for a lovely evening, gave him a chaste peck on the cheek, and leaving him in the foyer escaped to her room. Not long after, she was in a sound sleep filled with pleasant dreams.

Chapter 6
Was there ever another life?

Waking again to the sun streaming through the window, she felt as if this was the life she had always known.

It seemed unbelievable that only a few short weeks ago she had been preparing to be homeless, in a dull, grey, city, having lost her job, her family and her humdrum existence.

Now the day beckoned, full of promise. Her mind was ready to take on the challenge of the new experiences that the day would hold; seeing new things, learning about the history, meeting new people and enjoying life to the full in the comfort and luxury of her new surroundings.

What had seemed at the time to be extravagant purchases now seemed practical. She was looking forward to browsing her new wardrobe to find the right outfit for her sightseeing day.

Full of beans she jumped out of bed, took a quick shower and selected another cool cotton dress to face the day.

Armed with her guidebooks, she enjoyed a continental breakfast and then caught the early hotel bus into town.

This time instead of heading towards the harbour she took the road leading into the old town. She found herself gazing at the wonderful architecture of the old Auberge described in her guidebook.

Going into the cool of the building and paying the small entrance fee, she had expected her visit to only last half an hour or so. Instead, the deceptively spacious building led her into more and more rooms, all full of historical interest, until with a start, she realised it was already gone midday.

After the coolness of the museum's interior the sun seemed blinding when she emerged and she realised she was ready for a long cool drink.

Finding a local café nearby, she placed her order, and then started browsing through the leaflets and brochures she had picked up this morning at the museum.

Engrossed in her reading, it took her a moment to realise that someone was addressing her, asking if the other chairs at her table were free.

She noticed suddenly that the café had filled up with the lunchtime crowds and her table was the only one with spare places.

Moving her bags off the chair next to her, she realised that she recognised the group of five people from the dining room of her hotel on her first night.

It would have seemed rude to carry on reading with the others huddled round her table and before long they had all introduced themselves and she was included in their conversation.

She found out they all worked for the same company as a specialist team of researchers attached to a major tourist industry group, providing reports and information on little known areas and exclusive hotels for the wealthier clients.

Even though they were on their break, she soon found that she was being subtly grilled as to her opinion of the hotel, which of the facilities she had used, what were her particular impressions and likes and dislikes from what she had seen so far.

She realised that they had mistakenly assumed that she was an experienced, self-sufficient traveller, and her preferences would be similar to their target market.

By the time they went their separate ways, she had promised to meet up at the hotel to spend the evening with them, and see something of the local nightlife.

She couldn't make up her mind if she was looking forward to spending the evening in their company. Although they were all pleasant enough and Paul, in particular, seemed to be quite taken with her, it was not in her nature to make friends on first meeting.

In fact, even though she didn't like to admit it, even to herself, most of the people she classed as friends were actually just acquaintances, work colleagues, friends of her sisters, or people she had known from college.

She decided to go back to the hotel, rest for a while, have an early dinner and then decide whether she would meet them or make some excuse.

Decision made, she collected up her belongings and walked to the pick-up point, to get the courtesy bus which was due shortly.

Arriving at the bus point with about ten minutes to spare, she took advantage of a convenient bench, sat down and raised her face to feel the warmth of the sun. Feeling herself squinting, she put on her new designer sunglasses and laid back, enjoying the gentle breeze blowing in from the sea, which stopped it from being unbearably hot.

Back at the hotel she felt surprisingly tired, so slipping off her outer clothes, she lay back on the bed to rest her eyes for a few minutes and was soon fast asleep.

Opening her eyes suddenly, she realised that the sun was already going down and she had slept for nearly an hour.

Jumping up, she had a quick reviving shower, washed her hair, then went to examine her wardrobe to see what would be suitable to wear that night.

Unsure where they would end up, she settled on an angel sleeved, knee length, silky, cotton dress with an abstract blue pattern, and low heeled navy blue sandals.

Although not the sort of outfit she would usually wear at home, it seemed perfect for the evening, whether they ended up in a disco, smart hotel, or sitting outside somewhere watching the world go by.

After putting on some make-up, including some blue mascara, which brought out the colour of her dress, she added some jewellery, grabbed a light silky shawl, in case it turned chilly later, and she was ready.

Chapter 7
New friends

As it was still quite early for dinner by continental standards, the dining room was fairly empty and although she didn't rush her meal, she still had some time to kill before the hour she had agreed to meet her new friends.

Undecided whether to return to her room for a while or not, she passed a ladies' powder room and decided she would just use that to freshen up a bit.

As she emerged a few minutes later, a large empty lounge area caught her attention and she decided to wait there.

Settling herself in one of the comfortable bucket chairs round a small table near the door, she would have a good view of anyone coming through the foyer where they had arranged to meet but the partially open door obscured her from view of the casual passer-by.

Despite the modern, well-stocked bar at the end of the room to her right, there was a feel of historical luxury in the beautifully ornate oak furniture and the flocked wall coverings. The large sliding doors opening onto the gardens and the sheer size of the room, gave it an open airy feel despite the heavy furniture.

A slight movement drew her attention to a small raised area opposite the bar, and diagonally across from where she was sitting. As it was next to a grand piano, she assumed it was some sort of stage for accompanying musicians to place their instruments, or to enable an audience to have a better view of a vocalist.

What fascinated her was the appearance from under the dais of the bottom of a shoe, closely followed by another shoe and heel, and a pair of jean-clad legs moving slowly backwards.

Finally a slim waist, broad shouldered T-shirt and the back of a dark haired head emerged. Although he was still stretched full out, she realised that she was looking at a tall, well-built man, presumably a workman of some sort.

Standing up and shaking his head to clear some clinging cobwebs, it was a moment until he turned round and noticed that she was watching him.

He gave a wry grin and her first thought was how good-looking he was, despite the covering of dirt and dust from under the floorboards.

"Sorry," he said, "I didn't expect to find anyone in here. Did you want a drink or something?"

Feeling rather embarrassed and wondering if she should be in there, she called back, "No, I'm fine. I'm just waiting for some friends."

Turning to the empty bar she saw his grin change to a frown. "There should be someone serving. Perhaps he just popped out. Let me just wash up a bit. I'll be back in a minute."

Before she could protest, he had disappeared through a door behind the bar and out of sight.

She wondered if she should just go and wait somewhere else but from his comments about the missing barman, she assumed the lounge was actually open to guests and she wasn't intruding.

She heard the distant sound of running water from behind the bar area. A few minutes later he returned with a laden coffee tray and after grabbing a bottle from behind the bar as he was passing, headed towards her table.

"Do you mind if I join you for a few minutes?" he asked as he deposited the tray on the table and took the seat opposite her. "I could do with a break."

Feeling like a tongued-tied young schoolgirl on her first date, she merely nodded her acceptance and watched as he poured them both a liquor and coffee, then stretched back in the chair.

"Do you work here?" she asked, almost for the sake of something to say, then felt herself blushing as that wry grin crossed his face again.

Mentally she berated herself. What a stupid question. Would he be under the floorboards and serving drinks from the bar if he was just a guest?

"You could say that," he smiled. "I was just checking out a faulty connection. I don't know what happened to James, he should still have been behind the bar, even if there were no customers. By the way, I'm Reno."

"Jane," she replied. "Nice to meet you."

His handshake was warm and strong and again she felt the girlish ripples running up her spine.

Within a very short time they were chatting easily, like old friends.

'Wow, he's really something,' she thought to herself. 'I could go for him in a big way, but knowing my luck he's probably married with a beautiful wife and six kids.'

She realised that although he had found out that she was single, had been made redundant recently from her job and was alone on an open-ended holiday, he hadn't really given away a lot about his own personal life.

She was sure he was just going to ask her out when they both heard a noise from the room behind the bar and glancing at his watch, he jumped up asking her to excuse him for a minute. She heard the sound of muted but angry voices and assumed the missing James was being given a ticking off for deserting his post.

Just then Paul poked his head round the doorway calling, "There you are. Come on, they're all waiting," grabbed her by the hand and hauled her out to the waiting car.

She hardly had time to glance back and wasn't even sure if Reno had noticed her going.

Chapter 8
The morning after

Paul and the others had proved good company and she had enjoyed herself the previous night, even though every now and again she found herself, probably unfairly, comparing Paul to Reno.

Although he was good looking and charming, he didn't give her the tingle that even hearing Reno's deep voice gave her.

'That guy would sound sexy just reading the phone book,' she thought to herself.

She must have let the sun go to her head.

She had only talked to Reno for less than an hour, and knew nothing about him except his first name. Even that was probably a nickname and it was quite likely that she wouldn't even see him again.

If he was some sort of general hotel repair man he would be spending all his time either in the non-public areas, or carrying out minor repairs in private rooms.

She remembered that she had arranged to meet Paul and the others for a late lunch, as they were flying out that evening.

As it was still early, she decided to try out some of the hotel's facilities and spend the morning by the pool. Grabbing her swimming things, sunglasses and a book, she headed off to find the outdoor pool then found herself wondering if the pool ever needed any minor repairs.

After berating herself for being so childish, she spent a peaceful couple of hours on a sun lounger, moving it round now and then to get some shade when she got too hot, and then back into the sun after her frequent short swims, to help dry off.

When she went back to her room to shower and change before lunch, she noticed that she had now acquired a tan, except for the small area that had been covered by the tiny bikini that she had actually got up the nerve to wear by the pool.

Again she enjoyed herself with the crowd over lunch and felt that she would actually miss them now that they were leaving.

Paul had insisted that she take his mobile number and look him up whenever they happened to be in the same country but she had managed to avoid giving him hers without causing offence.

She went down to the foyer to wave them off when they left the hotel around five that evening, then found herself at a loss as to what to do next.

There wasn't time to go into town before dinner but it was too early to start getting ready for the evening yet.

Momentarily she thought of ringing Greg but then decided that wouldn't be fair.

It had been fun with Paul, as part of the crowd, but she had the feeling that Greg would think she was offering more than just a dinner 'à deux' if she contacted him first.

Almost as if he had read her thoughts, she was handed a message as she passed back through reception. Greg had phoned again.

Would she possibly be free to join him for drinks with some business contacts that evening? They were having a working dinner but later his colleagues would be joined by their wives and girlfriends and he didn't want to be the 'spare man.'

Making her decision before she had time to change her mind, she used the phone in the foyer to confirm yes, she would be free and arranged for him to collect her from the hotel about 9.30.

Making her way to the hotel restaurant shortly before 8, she was again given what she had come to think of as 'her' table and enjoyed a pleasant meal on her own.

Greg arrived dead on time and although, at first, she was somewhat embarrassed when it was assumed that she was Greg's long-standing girlfriend, she soon relaxed in the congenial company and the evening passed quickly.

Even when she refused his offer of a nightcap in her room, Greg took it well and she was happy to join him for a late night drink in the safety of the hotel's bar.

The goodnight kiss he gave her outside her door confirmed that he wanted to be more than friends. When she refused to let him come in to say goodnight properly, he said he forgave her on condition she would spend his final day with him.

Laughing she agreed and arranged to meet him around 9.30 the following morning.

Chapter 9
More goodbyes

Jane woke the next morning after a restless night, disturbed by the mixed up dream she had been having.

In the dream she had been with Paul but surrounded by Greg's friends, whilst Paul himself was behind the bar being told off by Mark for not looking after his guests.

She assumed that the shadowy figure watching must have been Reno, although his face wasn't clear.

As she was finishing her breakfast she remembered Mark being in the dream. Guiltily she realised she hadn't contacted her sister since she left England.

No time now but she must remember to send her an e-mail when she got back that night.

Greg was waiting for her as she walked through the foyer just before 9.30, looking cool and relaxed in linen trousers and a pale blue short-sleeved shirt.

She realised it was the first time she had seen him not in a suit, and for some reason, it made him look younger and much more approachable.

He greeted her with a big smile and a kiss on the cheek, then took her hand to walk her out to the car.

She felt herself relaxing, and even found herself gently flirting with him when, in response to her query as to where they were going, he teasingly replied, "Wait and see."

After a short drive, they pulled up close to a marina where, amongst the small rowing boats, were a range of yachts, some of which she thought would cost more than the average house.

Again he took her hand to lead her down the wooden walkway and stopped next to one of the boats moored up.

Although not in the class of some she had noticed, nevertheless, it was luxurious, and she could imagine it being someone's pride and joy.

For a fleeting moment she did wonder if it belonged to Greg, but then she was being welcomed aboard by Mario, one of Greg's business associates she had met the night before. The pride with which Mario showed her round made it obvious it belonged to him.

His wife Maria emerged from the galley to greet her, then she was introduced to another, younger, couple she hadn't met before but who greeted her warmly.

Mario himself took the controls to steer them out of the harbour, assisted by the crew who, she soon discovered, were his daughter and son-in-law.

Luckily she had thought to bring her bikini, although not the tiny one she had worn the previous day. Soon she was relaxing on deck, feeling the cool breeze blowing through her hair, helping to counteract the warmth of the blazing sun.

The motion of the boat on the waves was like a lullaby and she was worried that she would drift off to sleep. Not a very sociable thing to do she thought, so she was pleased when after an hour or so Mario steered the boat towards a small island and moored up.

The crystal-blue water looked so inviting that it didn't take long for them all to take the plunge and go for a swim.

After the heat of the sun, the cool of the water was almost a shock but she soon warmed up again with the exercise and realised that it was in fact pleasantly warm.

Once they had dried themselves in the sun, the six of them set off to explore the island, still clad in their swimwear, as were most of the other visitors they came across on their walk. An hour of clambering over the rocks made her feel the muscles in the backs of her legs start to ache, and she realised that she had got lazy since she left England.

All this good living was starting to take its toll. She made a mental note that when she got to the hotel she would have to check if they had a gym.

The views from some of the high points were spectacular and she was intrigued when Mario pointed out some of the wild birds hidden in the bushes and shrubs, which she would have missed were it not for his sharp eyes.

She was even more amazed when after another rigorous climb he led her to a small but deep hidden seawater pool, and pointed out the tiny multi-coloured fish that had been stranded by the tides.

After all the unaccustomed exercise, she realised she was ravenous. Maria and her daughter had prepared a sumptuous cold buffet which they ate on deck, washed down by a few bottles of cool, chilled, white wine.

Overcoming their protests, she helped the women clear up while the men took the boat out again into deeper water and anchored some way off shore.

This time she didn't feel so bad about stretching out on deck and lazing sleepily in the sun as the others were all doing the same.

In between dozing they chatted quietly and she felt that she could happily spend the rest of her life like this, especially if she was lying next to a tall, dark-haired man with a deep voice and a wry smile.

Immediately she felt ashamed of herself. Greg had been the perfect companion, affectionate but not pushy and after trying so hard to make her happy, she wasn't being fair to him by letting another man intrude into her thoughts.

Maybe because she felt guilty she over-compensated by being particularly affectionate with Greg but then felt guilty again that she might be giving out the wrong signals.

Despite her private thoughts it had been a perfect day and she genuinely liked Greg and felt his friends couldn't have treated her better if she had actually been his wife, rather than a chance acquaintance.

She was really sorry the day had to end and after he had dropped her back at her hotel, prior to packing for his evening flight, it was she who suggested that, if he had time, he drop by on the way to the airport for a final drink together.

The smile on his face when he enthusiastically agreed, almost made her want to retract her words, in case he read too much into it but it was too late now.

It was only when he did call at her hotel about 8 for a final drink to say goodbye, that the pleasure on his face when he saw her waiting, made her glad she had actually suggested it.

When his cab arrived to take him to the airport he kissed her goodbye tenderly and she found herself meaning it when she gave him her mobile number and promised to keep in touch when she got back to England.

The only thing that spoilt it was that she had to keep forcing herself not to look back at the bar area as they had their goodbye drink in the lounge where she had first seen Reno.

Not unexpectedly, he didn't make an appearance, although she couldn't stop her eyes drifting towards the stage where she had first seen him emerge, especially when a three-piece band started playing around 8.30.

After Greg reluctantly left, she felt she couldn't face dinner in the hotel dining room alone.

At a loss as to what to do she left the hotel and wandered aimlessly for a while. She found herself walking along the coast road and being attracted by a sign outside an old-fashioned wooden restaurant, set on the beach, proudly announcing 'Gino's'.

While she was dithering outside, a wrinkled old man, old enough to be her grandfather but still with a twinkle in his eye, came out to greet her. Before she knew it she had been ushered inside and he was showing her the menu, explaining that everything was fresh and homemade, and the best food she would ever taste on the island.

Half laughing, she was still quite relieved when an elderly lady, obviously his wife, berated him for a few minutes in their own language, then switching to English asked if she would like a private table overlooking the sea.

Agreeing that sounded wonderful, she was led through wooden dividing doors into what she had assumed was a private part of the restaurant. It turned out to be a small terrace, actually on the beach, with a small table for two at each end, separated by a wooden dividing screen in the middle.

Wanting to be alone with her thoughts but at the same time not wanting to be cut off from company, this was the perfect solution.

She could hear the sound of the main part of the restaurant rapidly filling up but her position behind the wooden half door made it possible for her to see and hear without getting involved.

Gino and his wife seemed to have taken her under their wing, as if she was a favourite granddaughter. In between serving customers they kept popping back to see if she was alright, whether she wanted anything, and how was her meal?

Wasn't it true it was the freshest she had ever tasted?

Laughing she was happy to agree it was indeed.

In between their visits she was happy to look out over the dark horizon and listen to the waves gently crashing onto the shore not many yards from where she was sitting.

The muted background noise coming from the restaurant made the peace and tranquillity of the sea even more inviting. She found herself just listening to the sounds of the night and enjoying the freedom of being alone.

She was just reluctantly thinking she should pay her bill and return to the hotel when her attention was caught by a deep voice which seemed to be coming from the restaurant near the kitchen area.

Unable to help herself she listened unashamedly to the conversation.

Even from her hide-away she could hear the affection in their voices as Gino and his wife scolded the newcomer for the length of time that had passed since his last visit.

'Was he ashamed of them? Why wasn't he bringing a nice lady for them to meet?'

'Wasn't it about time he settled down, got married to a decent girl and raised a family for them to love as their own grandchildren?'

She heard the loving teasing in his voice as he replied, "Give me time, when I find her you will be the first to know."

For a moment she panicked as she realised she was being discussed as the lovely lady, sitting alone on the terrace, who would be perfect for him. "Come, let me introduce you."

With a sigh of relief she heard him say, "Another time." At the moment he just wanted to sit alone and watch the sea.

She heard a chair scrape back on the other side of the dividing screen, then silence until Gino's wife returned a short while later to speak to him again.

Although she could not understand the language, it was obvious that she had brought him a plate of food and was urging him to eat and enjoy it. She sensed, as much as heard, the affectionate kiss on the old lady's cheek, then silence again, apart from the rattle of cutlery and now and again the chink of a glass being lifted.

Was it really Reno, or was her overactive imagination just going into overdrive.

She wasn't sure if she wanted to know the answer. Imagine her disappointment if she caught a glimpse of the stranger and he turned out to be an overweight, balding, middle-aged man who actually was the grandson of this lovely couple.

Even more embarrassing, what if they tried to pair them off as the perfect couple?

How could she refuse without insulting them after all their kindness to her?

Making her decision she jumped up and edged her way back into the main restaurant, taking care not to be visible from the screen.

Finding Maria, Gino's wife, with her hands full, she took advantage of the situation, thrusting some money into her apron pocket, which she hoped would be enough to cover the cost of her meal plus a generous tip. She kissed her briefly on her cheek and promised to come back soon, saying the meal had been wonderful.

She successfully made her escape out of the restaurant to the safety of the coast road, almost running until she was out of sight and then slowed down and walked at a leisurely pace until she reached her hotel.

Collecting her key from the receptionist, she wished him goodnight, and retreated back to her room. Now safely hidden, she almost felt ashamed of her hasty retreat but hadn't felt up to facing Reno again, if it had ever actually been him.

What was wrong with her she thought, first she was mooning over the guy, then ducking and diving to try to avoid seeing him and insulting a very sweet couple in the process.

She made a promise to herself that she would go back to the restaurant and make some excuse for her hasty departure, perhaps inventing that she had received a phone call from some friends who were waiting for her to join them urgently.

Before drifting off to sleep she realised that, unbelievably, less than a week ago she was still in London.

Although the days had passed quickly her old life felt as if it had been a lifetime ago and she still hadn't contacted her sister!

Chapter 10
A normal day

When Jane woke the next morning her mind was more focussed, as if she were her old efficient self.

After her bath she opened up her laptop and started preparing to send an e-mail to her sister. What to say? All of a sudden her mind had gone blank again and she had become the dizzy blonde socialite with her only thoughts of what to wear and where to spend the day.

Eventually she managed to get her brain working enough to compose an e-mail saying she was enjoying her holiday, had met lots of interesting people, seen some fascinating sights and was acquiring a suntan.

Even to herself it sounded stilted and reticent but it would have to do. She finished by asking how her sister was enjoying her new life and telling her to send lots of photos of their new home, just for the sake of something to say.

Shutting down her computer she realised that apart from having breakfast she had no plans for the day. With all her new friends now having deserted her, she would be once again left to her own devices.

It was almost a relief when she bumped into Bert and Martha when entering the dining room, and joined them at their table to share breakfast together.

They had booked a coach tour to visit some local historical ruins. She went to wave them off but when the tour guide readily accepted her last minute booking, the decision was made; she would spend the day with the elderly couple visiting ancient monuments.

Despite herself, she actually enjoyed the day.

She had always been interested in history and it was a relief to not have to worry about how she looked, or to have to watch what she said in case she was giving the wrong impression.

She could let Bert flirt with her, knowing that after so many years together, there was no way Martha would take offence.

The local guide had an extensive knowledge of his subject and the enthusiasm with which he answered questions showed that this was not just a job but a passion.

Returning to the hotel about 5 o'clock, she was happy to agree to the suggestion that she meet up again with Bert and Martha for the cabaret, which was to be held on the roof terrace later that evening.

As they liked an early evening meal, she found herself alone at her usual table to enjoy a solitary dinner.

When she went up to the roof at about 8.45 she was immediately spotted by the couple, who waved her over to join them at their table in a prime position close to the stage.

The tall, dark and handsome young singer reminded her of Reno. Bert and Martha were delighted when, despite their age difference, he picked on her as his special lady for the evening, serenading her and dancing with her on stage to 'Lady in Red', even though her dress was a pale turquoise.

She didn't linger for long after Bert and Martha went off to bed about 11.30, merely returning the blown kiss to her young admirer who was packing up his equipment but she still felt herself smiling after another happy but different day.

Chapter 11
Red faced and sunburnt

Jane stretched and woke with a smile still on her face. The more normal previous day had helped her put things into perspective and returned her to the reality of normal life, rather than the dream world in which she had existed for the last week.

The response to her e-mail to her sister was also full of normal things.

Mark was going for an interview for a job; they had been house hunting and thought they had found the perfect place. Now they were just waiting for the legal procedures and relying on their English bank to handle the transfer of funds efficiently so they could put down a deposit.

How was Jane managing on her own? Did she find the foreign food affected her?

Make sure to put on plenty of sunscreen so she didn't get sunburnt as she was not accustomed to the heat, was she feeling lonely with no one to talk to?

Thinking back over the time since she had been here and realising that she hadn't lacked male companionship for a single day, she was tempted to tell her sister all about the many admirers she had encountered.

Instead she reverted to her old self and merely replied that no, she was not lonely, she had met a lovely old couple, spent some evenings with them, had visited some interesting museums and was getting a tan from sitting in the sun by the pool in the hotel.

All of this was actually true but didn't explain the full story.

Still feeling as if she was two people inhabiting one body, she thought about the day ahead and how she would spend it.

Which side of her personality would emerge today, the bikini-clad, yacht-going beauty, or the staid, demure, lonely spinster, seeking out the company of people old enough to be her grandparents so she could feel comfortable.

A peaceful day on her own, she decided – not that she had much choice.

Maybe a trip to the Maritime museum she had noticed by the harbour, followed by some sunbathing.

Collecting her faithful tote bag, she headed for breakfast and then went to wait for the early morning courtesy bus.

When she reached the town, she spent a while wandering around some of the narrower side streets and looking in the windows of the tiny, family run, shops.

Passing an open door, she could feel the heat blazing out and peering through the doorway, she saw it was an old-fashioned bakery with a traditional oven that she thought could only now be found in a museum.

Noticing her standing by the door, the white coated, red-faced baker gave her a cheerful wave and beckoned her in to the shop.

Although she had only been curious and hadn't intended to buy anything, the smell of the fresh baked bread was so enticing she ended up with a paper bag containing two fresh rolls and a small local speciality pie, that the baker had insisted she must try.

In another bag was a pastry confection, brimming with nuts and fruit that she hadn't been able to resist.

Continuing her stroll along the street, she saw the dim interior of what appeared to be a grocery store. Pushing aside the curtain she was amazed at the variety of goods stacked from floor to ceiling inside the small shop.

She was greeted with a toothless smile from an old woman who, despite the heat, was wrapped from head to foot in a long black dress, with a fringed shawl draped around her shoulders.

Although the old lady's English was limited, Jane was soon the possessor of a small portion of peppered cheese, a few slices of delicious looking ham carefully wrapped in greaseproof paper, a glass bottle of fresh orange juice and a plastic bottle of water.

The business transaction completed and the cash carefully stored in a small wooden drawer under the counter, the old lady seemed loath to let Jane go.

Between hand signals, broken English and a mixture of words she didn't understand, Jane was grilled as to how many children she had, where was she staying, was she enjoying her holiday, and where did she live?

Recognising the word London, the old lady broke into more beaming smiles. Jane was amused when she finally understood that the woman's second cousin lived in London so of course Jane must know her!

Despite her best efforts, Jane was unable to make the old lady appreciate just how densely populated London was. Finally she left the shop after promising that if she should bump into her cousin when she got home, she would, of course, pass on the old lady's regards.

She was almost afraid to look into any more shops for fear she would end up buying even more food for lunch, or else spend the whole day inside dark shops talking to even more old people.

Taking an even smaller side turning, she negotiated a flight of broken steps, which was the main pavement between overhanging buildings. They seemed to have been carved out of the rock itself, leading her back to the civilisation of the main shopping area.

The heat of the sun after the shade of the back streets hit her with unexpected force and for a while she took refuge in the air-conditioned comfort of one of the modern stores.

After browsing for a while she discovered a tourist information area and emerged with a handful of leaflets, including a small map of the local area, giving the location of the various places of interest.

She didn't need the map to find her way to the harbour. The smell of the sea, the slight aroma of fish and the wheeling birds, scavenging overhead, were sufficient to head her in the right direction.

The salty smell grew stronger as she got closer and she noticed the number of cats emerging from shady places to snatch up the bones and leftovers from the fishermen's catches.

The Maritime museum was small but fascinating. She spent an hour looking at the old pictures and reading the stories of the various shipwrecks and legends of the local area.

Exiting via the souvenir shop, she couldn't resist buying a small, beautifully decorated, shell box, although she had no idea what she would do with it.

She was also tempted by the range of tiny glass animals and birds but reluctantly let common sense guide her, as they would most likely get broken before she could get them home.

For a moment she felt a pang of panic when she remembered that she didn't actually have a home any more. The nearest thing to it was her hotel room and she couldn't stay there forever.

Before she could get despondent, she walked back into the sunshine and sat for a while on a bench, watching the fishermen hauling up their catch and repairing their nets.

After a while she resumed her walk and took the steps down to the beach. Kicking off her shoes, she felt the warmth of the sand under her toes, and with the fresh sea air blowing through her hair, her usual good humour was soon restored.

She found the perfect spot and soon had her towel spread out over the sun lounger, with her belongings in the shade of the umbrella next to her.

She was amazed at the slim young lad who had manoeuvred the furniture into position for her.

He didn't look old or strong enough to lift anything but had handled the heavy, awkward, chair and brolly with ease, accepting the small tip she had given him with a big smile of thanks.

A large family group were a short distance from her, with the older members of the family sheltering under two or three umbrellas, keeping a watchful eye on two babies sleeping in their pushchairs. Meanwhile the younger ones and the children played ball on the beach, running, yelling and laughing, in and out of the clear blue water.

Opening her book she settled down to read for a while, looking up every now and then to watch the youngsters playing, or gaze out at the small boats bobbing about further out.

At one stage a large open-decked tourist boat sailed past quite close to the shore and she couldn't resist returning the waves of the smiling people on board.

Returning to her book, her attention was again distracted by the sight of a speedboat pulling a skier a bit further out.

Initially the teenager on the skis was handling them expertly, but she couldn't help laughing when, after trying to show off to the cheering girls on the speed boat, he took a spectacular tumble and had to be dragged unceremoniously back on board.

With the sun starting to beat down on her she decided to take a cooling dip herself.

For a moment she was a bit apprehensive about leaving her belongings on the beach but with the family group close by, for some reason she felt comfortable that they would keep an eye on them for her, should anyone stray too close.

The cool of the water felt heavenly and for a while she just drifted about, letting the waves take her, then floated in the shallower water nearer the beach.

In an effort to work off some of the excess weight she must have put on during the last week, she did put some energy into swimming properly for a while but all the exercise only made her realise that she was now hungry.

Shaking herself off, she returned to her lounger and unpacked the lunch she had bought earlier. The orange juice was still fairly cool and was so refreshing that before she realised it, the bottle was empty.

The fresh rolls, cheese and ham, soon followed suit and feeling replete, she lay back on the lounger and let her eyes drift closed.

Although she was aware of the noises in the background, they were comforting rather than disturbing and she just enjoyed the sensation of being totally lethargic.

She felt a slight bump and opened her eyes to see a beach ball rolling next to her chair. She heard a small voice with a delightful accent calling out, "Sorry, lady, sorry." With a smile she threw the ball back to the young girl, then, feeling hot again, she decided to have another dip before applying some lotion.

As she entered the water the same ball bounced close to her. Swimming towards it she threw it back to the group playing in the water.

Before she knew it she had become involved in their game and spent the next twenty minutes chasing and throwing and generally frolicking about like a teenager.

Finally exhausted, she threw the ball one last time then waved to the group as she went back to her chair to dry off. She applied some cream to her skin, which despite being in the sea, was beginning to feel quite hot and dry.

Although the bottle of water was by now quite warm, she gulped it greedily then moved the lounger round slightly more towards the sun, raising the backrest so she could sit up comfortably.

For a while she read some more of her book but mainly she just sat and gazed at the sea and watched the world go by.

Noticing a small beach café a short way away, she picked up her bag and slipping on a light cover-up over her bikini, made her way towards it. She selected a seat at a table next to the railing overlooking the beach and ordered a coffee, with another bottle of cold water to take back to the beach with her.

After using the toilets, she returned to her lounger and settled herself down again for another session of doing nothing in particular.

When she saw the family group start to collect up their things prior to leaving, she glanced at her watch and was surprised to see that the day had flown by and it was already 5 o'clock.

Finishing off the second bottle of water, she prepared to leave as well, stopping at a litterbin to drop off the remnants of her lunch.

Not sure she had the energy or inclination to walk back to the hotel bus pick-up point, she passed a line of waiting taxis and after giving the driver the name of her hotel, settled back to ride home in comfort.

As she entered the foyer she saw Bert and Martha sitting on a settee surrounded by their luggage and realised that they were going home that day.

Despite her protests that she had just come from the beach they insisted that she join them for coffee while they waited for their transport to the airport.

Accepting the inevitable she joined them, taking care that her still sandy skin didn't brush against their travelling clothes.

Although they had enjoyed every minute of their anniversary trip, she could tell that they were looking forward to getting home and seeing their children and grandchildren again.

Suddenly she remembered the pretty shell box she had bought, and on impulse dug it out of her bag and gave it to Martha as a small memento.

She was taken aback at the emotion in the old lady's eyes when she thanked her profusely for the lovely thought and despite being dressed in her Sunday best, insisted on giving her a big hug and kiss.

Coming out of her embrace she heard Martha telling someone behind her how kind and wonderful she was. Looking up, she found herself gazing straight into the eyes of Reno. She was aware of both his deep voice answering Martha and the strange look on his face but was unable to say a word, just feeling mortified that when she had finally seen him again she was grubby and dishevelled from her day on the beach.

The next few minutes passed in a flurry of activity as the couple's transport arrived and in between having their luggage loaded and final goodbye hugs, she didn't look at Reno again.

After a final goodbye wave to Bert and Martha, she took advantage of the fact that he had gone out to the waiting car with them and escaped back to her room.

Chapter 12
Alone but not lonely

Taking a long cool bath, she wasn't sure whether her red face was from her day in the sun, or her embarrassment at seeing Reno in such circumstances.

Her skin was now turning a golden brown and her blonde hair seemed to have got even paler, making her blue eyes look huge.

She applied copious amounts of expensive lotion to her skin to counteract the effect of the beating it had taken that day, then slipped on a loose, flowing, cotton caftan without bothering about underwear.

Feeling the beginnings of a headache, probably from too much sun, she lay down on the bed and closed her eyes.

Waking an hour and a half later, the headache was gone but she didn't feel up to getting dressed for dinner. Remembering the hotel brochure she perused the menu and placed her order for room service.

Answering the knock on her door about half an hour later, she tipped the waiter who had delivered her meal and lifted the covers off the plates to reveal an appetising selection of hot and cold, buffet style, antipasti, chicken and salads and fresh fruit, together with a complimentary half bottle of wine.

For the first time since she had been here, she found the remote control and settled down to eat while watching the TV.

Having been out of touch with world events for a while, she enjoyed catching up with both local and international news, then, flipping through the channels, found a film just starting that she had wanted to see for ages.

When the film finished she turned off the TV, yawned and stretched and before very long was back in bed and sound asleep.

Chapter 13
A day of contrasts

She woke the next morning feeling refreshed and somewhat ashamed of herself for the way she had reacted at seeing Reno again.

After all, she reasoned, with the hotel so close to the sea it was natural that people would come back from the beach in the late afternoon or early evening and anyway, what made her think he had any interest in her personally.

She remembered how he had been so pleasant with Bert and Martha and thought it was probably just his job to be nice to people.

Digging through her bag, she found the tourist brochures she had picked up the previous day and perused what was on offer.

One all day tour particularly attracted her attention as it seemed to take in most of the island. So far she had only seen her immediate area.

Phoning the number on the leaflet, she found that yes, the tour was running today, yes they did have a spare seat and she would be picked up at 9.30 by minibus to be taken to the coach departure point.

Quickly showering, dressing and packing her bag for the day, she went down for breakfast and was ready and waiting when the minibus arrived.

She was joined in the bus by a small group she hadn't seen before. After exchanging good mornings with them, she found herself, as the only single passenger, seated next to the driver, who chatted to her while driving to the coach station.

When she boarded the coach, she took a seat just in front of the back row and shortly afterwards they were off. The coach was only half full, and after introducing herself, the courier requested that they returned to the same seats after each stop, to make it easier to ensure that no-one had been left behind.

As this meant that she had no immediate neighbours, Jane listened to the running commentary when they went through places of interest, and spent the rest of the time looking out of the window.

Their first stop, at around 11 o'clock, was at a prehistoric ruin and she enjoyed wandering around the ancient stones imagining how different the existence of the people who had lived there must have been from her own.

She was back at the coach in good time for the next stage of their journey which included a short stop at a beauty spot reached by a road that was so narrow and winding she wondered what would happen if they met a coach coming the other way.

The view however, was well worth it; a panoramic vista of a wooded area with some small buildings just visible between the trees, leading to steep path strewn cliffs and finally down to the sea, crashing onto the rocks way below them.

After another short drive they arrived at the centre of a small, pretty, village where they were told they would be having lunch.

From their stopping point, a short walk took them to a surprisingly large hotel, where after walking through a shady courtyard, surrounded by flowers, they were shown to tables set out around the swimming pool for a barbecue style lunch.

Although they had to collect their own meat or fish from the extensive grill spread all along one side, they were served at their tables with salads, bread and bottles of wine, which she noticed were quickly replenished as they emptied.

The meal was finished off with a light mousse dessert and coffee and they were entertained by a small group, doing traditional dances and singing folk songs while they ate.

Then they were free to wander around at will, provided they were back at the coach by 3 p.m.

Glad of the chance to stretch her legs and clear her head after the unaccustomed lunchtime wine, Jane followed the line of people headed back towards the village.

She wandered around, taking in the very old buildings and souvenir shops, most of which appeared to have previously been the front parlours of the small houses.

Outside one group of homes she stopped to watch several old ladies, dressed in traditional black, with lace shawls covering their heads, sitting on rickety wooden chairs in the doorways of their homes.

While their tongues were going nineteen to the dozen as they chatted and gossiped, their hands moved equally fast, holding small bobbins of coloured threads which they weaved in and out to create complicated lace patterns on the various delicate handkerchiefs, table cloths and pillow cases they were working on.

She was equally intrigued by the patterns, colours and variations of wrought iron railings, surrounding many of the balconies overhanging the first floor of the buildings. Both the lace and the ironwork showed the same dedication to detail and she thought to herself how sad it would be if these ancient crafts were overtaken by modern technology.

As it was getting on for 3, she made her way back to the coach, resumed her seat and after waiting for a few stragglers they were off again.

Retracing their way down the steep, winding, road they turned onto a more modern two-lane highway, before turning off again, to take a bumpy track through fields and farms that seemed to be leading nowhere.

Suddenly the path opened up into a large car park, next to which were two modern, glass buildings, one housing a café/restaurant and the other a large ceramics showroom.

Beyond these buildings were rows of what looked like tinned roof huts, which the courier explained were actually the 'factories' of various artisans carrying out their traditional crafts.

Wandering in and out of the tin huts, she saw that they housed a wide variety of goods, being manufactured using ancient tools which she could well believe had been handed down from father to son over the centuries.

Apart from the lace making which she had seen in the village, they were free to watch glass being blown and shaped in the time-honoured way, delicate filigree being shaped by hand into beautiful pieces of jewellery and wood being crafted and notched to form pieces of furniture.

In one of the larger buildings towards the back of the area, she saw huge blocks of the local honey coloured stone. Inside, stonemasons were cutting the blocks into smaller pieces to be made into everything from headstones for graves, to small carved animals, wishing wells and garden planters.

Glancing at her watch she saw that time had once again flown by and she started retracing her steps back towards the coach.

Having a few minutes to spare, she browsed around the shop next to the car park, which was doing a roaring trade selling all the wares that had been produced in the various units.

Taking her seat again on the coach, she noticed that nearly all her fellow passengers were laden down with carrier bags containing items they had bought in the craft village.

One man was carrying an enormous but beautifully carved wooden sailing ship, with the craftsmanship showing in every minute detail down to the steering wheel, rudder and even the tiny bunk beds for the crew, which could be seen through the portholes along the side of the ornately decorated ship.

She thought of all the love and time that must have been invested to create such a beautiful piece and prayed that it wouldn't get damaged when the man tried to transport it home, to take pride of place on his mantelpiece.

When she got back to the hotel she half wished she had made some purchases herself but then again the realisation came to her that she was without a home.

Checking her e-mails, she found one from her sister saying that their money had been transferred efficiently and they had placed a deposit on the house of their dreams. Again she had a feeling of homesickness but surprised herself by wondering what prices were like for property on the island that already she was beginning to think of as home.

A task for the next day she thought, just to look at a few estate agents windows and get an idea of what was available.

Dressing for dinner, she tried to decide whether to eat in the hotel dining room, or find somewhere else for her meal.

Eventually she decided that as she had hardly spoken to a soul all day, the more or less familiar faces of the hotel waiters might actually be preferable.

Taking her time over her meal, she enjoyed the mild flirtation of the waiters, and then sat back to enjoy the music of the singer-guitarist who started his set while she was finishing her dessert.

When he took a break she started to fell restless and decided to take a walk along the shore road to help her sleep.

As she was wandering along, with no particular destination in mind, she suddenly remembered her hasty departure from Gino's. Was it really only the day before yesterday? It felt like a lifetime ago.

Before she knew it she was standing outside the restaurant and plucking up her courage, pushed open the door, and went in.

Immediately she was engulfed in a bear hug by Gino himself, who wanted to know why she had taken so long to come back to see them, didn't she like their food, what could he get her to eat, something special, leave it to him.

He was quickly joined by Maria who exclaimed over her beautiful tan, then went into motherly mode to tell her to take care, she didn't want to ruin that beautiful skin with too much sun.

Jane was somewhat overwhelmed with the welcome she had received, as if she was a long lost granddaughter rather than just a customer who had only been there once. She started to apologise for her hasty departure last time she was here but was cut off before she could make any excuses.

Of course she was in demand, a beautiful lady like her would have so many admirers, such a pity she hadn't met their Reno, such a lovely boy, they would have been perfect together and made such lovely babies.

Half embarrassed, half laughing, she found herself thinking, what would it be like to be married to Reno? Having his children, and setting up home together?

Whoa, she was beginning to think like his grandparents, if that's who they were.

To change the subject she told them that she had just had a big meal at the hotel but would love to stay for a drink, if that was alright with them.

Before she knew it she was being ushered onto the balcony to the table she had been given before. This time the dividing screen had been removed and with the door to the restaurant open, she was able to see all along the veranda and even into the restaurant itself which was filling up rapidly.

With Gino and Maria regularly popping in and out for a chat she felt herself relaxing until the door opened and she heard a familiar deep voice say, "Hello," and being promptly berated for neglecting them for so long.

Before she knew it Reno had been dragged up to her table, forced down into the chair opposite hers, introductions made and they were alone with just a small table between them.

He seemed to have taken all the scolding in good part and with that same wry grin on his face, held out his hand to her, said "Pleased to officially meet you," and told her that when Maria and Gino joined forces, you just had to shut up and do as you were told.

He looked gorgeous in a light-coloured T-shirt and denim jeans; she felt her heart flipping as he smiled at her. Trying to regain her sophistication, she was taken aback when he said that although she looked beautiful in her evening finery, she had looked as good, or even more beautiful when he had seen her that afternoon.

Feeling her face flush and trying to change the subject, she asked how he knew Bert and Martha.

His reply that he was a romantic at heart and loved to see couples like them, who had devoted themselves to each other for all those years, enjoying themselves in his hotel, which caused her heart beat to flip once again.

Later, she would remember the conversation, especially 'his hotel', although if he had worked there for some time, it was not a particularly strange thing to say.

Trying to divert the attention away from her, she asked if he had been at the hotel for a long time and did he enjoy working there?

Again that enigmatic grin as he said 'yes', he had been based there since it opened under new management some five years ago, and 'yes', although there were some bad days, on the whole he was loving every minute, especially the opportunity to meet beautiful women travelling alone.

Feeling herself blushing again, Jane couldn't help thinking that a good-looking man like him would be able to pick and choose from the female clients, young or mature, who stayed at the hotel.

Noticing her glass was empty, he beckoned to Gino who was passing by and called for another drink for them both.

An hour or so later, after realising that he had devoted his total attention to her, asking about her life, her hopes and her dreams, Jane was just starting to believe that he wasn't the lothario she had first thought, when they were rudely interrupted. A young, expensively dressed, woman screamed his name and throwing her arms round him, protested in a loud voice that he had been neglecting her.

Gently taking the woman's arm, and excusing himself for a moment, he led her back into the main part of the restaurant. On the way he greeted the group she was with who obviously knew him well.

Glancing up, she caught the eye of the woman, who looked her up and down with a sneer on her face and then obviously dismissed her as being of no importance.

Not able to resist eavesdropping, she caught snatches of conversation including Daddy's yacht, parties and various unsubtle hints about sleeping over AGAIN.

Feeling humiliated and thinking this time HE could settle the bill, she made her escape down the back stairs leading to the beach. She kicked off her shoes and raced along the sand until she reached some steps leading back to the road, paused for a minute to put her shoes back on, and then almost ran back until she reached the hotel foyer.

Taking a deep breath to regain her composure, she collected her key from reception, said goodnight and retreated to the security of her hotel room, where she double-checked the lock on the door.

Chapter 14
What now? What next? Where to?

Oh God, was her first waking thought. Why is it that every time I see him I act like a stupid teenager?

Why can't I enjoy a drink in his company and then dismiss him from my thoughts, like a sophisticated woman of the world, until the next chance meeting.

Am I such a coward that I have to hide behind an impersonal locked hotel room door, just in case he happens to smile in my direction?

She almost wished that Paul or Greg were still around. At least with them she could relax, enjoy a mild flirtation and enjoy their obvious interest in her without feeling she was out of her depth.

She seriously considered whether it was time to arrange her flight home, check out of the hotel and get back to the reality of her old life in London.

If nothing else she could sign on to a temp agency, find a few days' work to get her brain working again, and relegate the last week to her memories as a holiday romance.

Reverting to her intelligent self, she thought that the brief meetings with Reno could not even be classified as a romance, although with a bit of embellishment her liaisons with Paul and Greg could be woven into an amusing, romantic, story with which to regale people.

That train of thought led her back to realising that actually she didn't have any close friends to tell the stories to and for a short while she even considered emigrating to Australia to join her sister.

Pulling herself together she knew that was not an option.

Jena had started her new life with her new husband and her new country. She would not welcome the intrusion of a spinster, lonely, sister disturbing her new world.

Determined to take back control of her life, she threw on the first clothes that came to hand, went down to breakfast, then caught the early shuttle service into town.

The shops and businesses were only just starting to open and when she found herself gazing into the window of an estate agent, she was immediately accosted by a middle-aged man who ushered her inside and started taking details, obviously keen to start the business day on a high note.

Before she knew it she was in his car, being driven to various locations to inspect a range of properties, from single bedroomed flats in high-rise blocks to an exclusive villa in the old part of town, complete with five bedrooms, swimming pool and gated entrance, with a price tag to match.

Thanking him for his time, she escaped a few hours later with her mind buzzing with facts and figures but knowing that nothing she had been shown so far had inspired her.

However, it had made her realise that overall, the prices on the island were far removed from London prices and that she could easily afford a small villa should she decide to stay.

Although she had no definite plans, that thought somehow brought her comfort and she tried to convince herself that it was nothing to do with the fact that she would be in the same part of the world as Reno, with the likelihood of bumping into him again.

Thinking of her stomach, she headed towards a small local café she had noticed when the estate agent had dropped her off.

Although the exterior was not impressive by tourist standards, the premises were clean, the welcome genuine and the food home cooked and delicious. Complimenting the owner on the excellent meal, she was immediately introduced to his wife 'Mama', the chef, who was effusive in her thanks and once again she began to feel like the long lost daughter.

I could actually live here, she thought as she paid her bill with the promise to visit again soon.

With nothing better to do, she took a long walk around a residential area she hadn't seen before but which, although in a back street, was close to all the amenities of the town centre.

Her attention was drawn to a gated house, hidden behind a high hedge, ensuring privacy from the road but still part of the community.

As she was gazing at the villa, an elderly man came out and greeted her in perfect English but with a strong accent, and asked her if she was interested in looking around.

At first she was surprised that the property was actually up for sale but then realised that she was not in London, where any available property would be inundated with For Sale signs.

Accepting his invitation, she let herself be led inside to a beautiful courtyard with the strong, sweet, smell of flowers, leading to an outdoor swimming pool, complete with a decking area and garden.

Going into the house she was enchanted by the airy, spacious, rooms, three bedrooms, two of which were en-suite, a modern bathroom complete with Jacuzzi, small box room, a separate shower room and toilet, a utility room, modern kitchen and even a rooftop terrace complete with barbecue to hold open air parties during the summer.

Although she was enchanted by the property, which already seemed like home, she couldn't believe that such a perfect place could be in her price range, so she was astounded when the offered opening price quoted to her was only half of what she expected.

Although still a bit above her budget, it was realistic for her to be able to afford.

Her enthusiasm and immediate rapport with the property must have been obvious and she was beginning to think about making him a serious offer.

Making a note of his details, she promised to be in touch soon.

While she was in the area, she took the opportunity to examine her immediate surroundings.

Taking a left turn she found herself in a tree lined road leading to a small square.

She noticed a baker's, butcher's and a general store selling all sorts of household equipment.

At the opposite side of the square were a greengrocer's, mini supermarket and even a hairdresser's, everything she could need, right on her doorstep.

On the road facing her, leading away from the square, she noticed there were a few bars and even a row of three restaurants. Turning the next corner she was again facing the sea, which she had been able to see from the terrace of the house.

Her mind buzzing, she made her way back to her hotel and asked the receptionist whether they had a local business directory, so she could start looking for some of the legal businesses she would need if she did pursue her dream and actually buy the property.

As it turned out, the receptionist was married to a notary and before she knew it, Jane had a business card giving the office address, which was not far from the harbour and an appointment booked for the next morning.

Thinking about her dinner that evening, she didn't want to return to Gino's for fear she would bump into Reno again but neither did she feel like staying in the hotel.

Making her decision to find somewhere new, she set off to walk into town, and without conscious thought, found herself fifteen minutes later near 'her' house.

She saw a building she hadn't noticed before that turned out to be a hotel, with a sign outside advertising a gym and beauty shop, open to non-residents.

'If I carry on eating the way I have been I will need to join that,' she thought to herself, then realised with a start that she was already acting as if she was living there and making plans for her future.

Taking the road leading to the square, she noticed that the restaurants she had seen earlier were now ablaze with lights.

Approaching them, one in particular caught her attention. Although not particularly big inside, it was surrounded by wide terraces, on which were tables and chairs, mainly in groups of twos and fours, but with one or two large tables that could comfortably hold six or eight.

Flowers were entwined all along the terracing, with more potted plants in odd nooks and crannies, their heady aromas mixed with the enticing smells wafting from the kitchen at the back of the restaurant.

She was greeted by a young girl who, after confirming that she was happy to sit outside, led her to a table for two on the terrace, took her drinks order and left her to browse the menu.

Looking around she was struck by the pretty effect created by the table settings.

Each table had a tablecloth, candlestick and napkins in a matching colour, some were blue, some yellow, some red and some green, spaced so that the colours contrasted and complemented each other.

Returning with her drink, the waitress asked if she had any special preferences, told her about the specials for the day and took the time to explain some of the more unusual items on the menu.

Being guided by the waitress's selection, she enjoyed an excellent meal, washed down with another half bottle of wine and finished with a liqueur to go with her coffee.

After chatting for a while with the friendly waitress once the main rush of dinners was over, she paid her bill and took a slow walk back along the coast road.

Stopping for a while on a bench facing the sea, she watched the tide lapping on the sand and felt that with the right person next to her this would be paradise.

Her thoughts turning as usual to Reno, she wondered who the woman from last night had been.

Thinking about it she realised that it was the woman who had made all the running. Reno himself had been polite but detached, and she resolved that next time, she would be mature and open, and find out if he really was at all interested in her.

'Chance would be a fine thing,' she thought to herself, she might never see him again.

Getting up and walking back to her hotel, she had a comparatively early night; her mind still spinning from the way the future seemed to be shaping itself.

Chapter 15
Legalese and more developments

The next morning, she dressed in a more conservative outfit to put her in the proper business mood, checked she had a notebook and pen in her bag and set off for her morning appointment.

She was greeted by the notary, Mr Borg, in perfect English and shown into a stylish modern office.

He was careful to ensure that she understood all the various processes involved, what the costs would be and how long things were likely to take to complete.

He had even spoken to the owners of the house and discovered that it would be vacant within two weeks, as the couple were moving in with their daughter, the house having become too much for them now that all their children had left home.

It was the notary's suggestion that she could rent it for a few months while the paperwork was being sorted out, which would give her time to decide if she was certain she wanted to make the island her home.

By paying them a small deposit, she could secure the property, and even if she did later change her mind, the sum she would lose would be negligible compared to the cost of staying in her current hotel or even renting elsewhere.

It was the perfect answer and before she could change her mind she had signed an initial agreement, promising to arrange for her bank to transfer the deposit funds as soon as was feasible.

She made a further appointment with him for a few days' time, when he would take her to the various government and utility offices to obtain the necessary permits and residential visas.

He assured her that although it was a grinding and slow process, as both her new and old countries were in the EU, there should not be any problems with her application and he would take care of all the paperwork.

All that was left for her to do was to ensure she had her passport with her when they next met and arrange to give him six up to date, passport-sized, photographs.

Her mind once again reeling from the speed with which things were happening, she did not at first register the deep voice greeting Mr Borg as she shook hands with him at the door of his office as she was saying goodbye.

Turning slowly she came face to face with Reno.

As the notary started making introductions he was interrupted by Reno saying, "We've met. Hello Jane, how are you?"

Determined this time to show him she did have more than one brain cell in her head, she took his offered hand and replied coolly, "I'm fine. Nice to see you again," as if they were old acquaintances.

She had no chance to refuse when, after Mr Borg offered to get her a taxi, Reno told him not to bother, he would only be a minute, then he would give her a lift.

With the door closed behind them she was tempted to run but chided herself for being foolish and to remember the promise she had made to herself, about how she would act if she ever saw him again.

She just hadn't expected it to be so soon, or in such circumstances.

True to his word, Reno emerged only a few minutes later, took her arm and led her to the rather ancient car parked outside.

"I've just got to make one stop-off on the way, then we can go and sort out your photographs," he told her as he started the car and they drove off.

Still feeling somewhat stunned, she sat in silence until he stopped outside a block of flats and invited her to come up with him while he dropped something off.

She was still in somewhat of a daze as he opened the communal door and led her up the stone steps to the first floor. She was even more surprised when, instead of knocking, he took a key out of his pocket and let himself in.

For a moment she panicked, assuming he had brought her back to his own flat and no-one would know where she was if he attacked her.

Then pulling herself together and thinking that the notary would not have greeted a homicidal maniac so cordially, she heard his voice calling her to take a seat while he disappeared through a door into another room.

"All done," he smiled as he came back to join her a few minutes later and refused his offer of a drink.

Again that enigmatic grin as he locked the door behind them, almost as if he had read her thoughts.

She had expected him to get back in the car but instead he took her hand and led her along the road, explaining that the photographer's studio was only just round the corner and it would be quicker to walk.

Half an hour later they emerged with Reno holding the folder of photographs, which he promised to drop off to Charles Borg, who he would be seeing again later.

Before she knew it, they were seated in a quiet corner of yet another small restaurant where he was warmly greeted as a regular customer.

It was only after he had ordered their meal, and a bottle of wine had been placed on their table, that he moved his chair round next to her, effectively blocking her way out.

"Now you can't escape," he told her, "until you explain why you run away every time I see you."

Her mind whirling with possible intelligent ways to answer, she was horrified when all that came out of her mouth was, "Who was that woman?"

Instead of being defensive, he seemed strangely pleased at her question and explained that she was the daughter of an old friend of his father's, and although she had a good heart, she could tend to be a bit over effusive.

"Next question?" he smiled.

"Are you married?" she blurted out.

"No, are you?"

"No."

"Now it's my turn," he smiled. "Any special man in your life?"

She was almost tempted to say 'only you' but the shyness overtook her again and she just gave a non-committal answer.

To change the subject she told him about her sister emigrating, her childhood home being sold and her decision to take a short holiday while she decided what she wanted to do.

He was a good listener and she was pleased when the waitress returned with their meal as she felt she had been giving away so many details of her life, without learning anything more about him, except that he wasn't married.

Although her meal was superb, his seafood pasta looked equally delicious and noticing her look, he was soon feeding her forkfuls from his plate, which she had the choice of either eating, or having it dropped in her lap.

The bottle of wine was starting to take effect and before she knew it, she was doing the same to him, laughingly stopping him asking questions as she force fed him portions of her excellent lasagne.

When he reluctantly told her that he had to leave soon, she thought her watch must have stopped as it showed it was already gone 5 o'clock, until she realised the heat of the day had started to turn into a warm, balmy evening.

Feeling suddenly sad that the day was ending, she felt her heart lift when he told her that although he would not be able to take her to dinner, he would be free to meet her at Gino's about 10 o'clock that night if she was free.

Assuring him she would be there, she refused his offer of a lift home as he was obviously running late but, despite his haste, he still waited until her taxi arrived and gave her a sweet kiss before waving her goodbye.

Turning to look out of the back window of the cab, she saw him hastily leaving some money on the table before waving to the waitress and almost running up the road.

With a pang, she wondered if she had made him late for work and also how much of his weekly salary he had blown on their meal.

Perhaps she should have offered to pay, or would that have been insulting?

She determined that when they met up later she would give Gino sufficient in advance to cover their bill so there could be no arguments.

Arriving at her hotel, she felt she was missing him already, although she had only left him about twenty minutes ago and couldn't wait to see him again in a few hours' time.

Preparing for the evening ahead, she changed her outfit four times before realising that time was slipping away and she needed to get to the dining room now if she was going to be ready in time to meet Reno.

She hardly noticed what she ate and after freshening up, she was soon hurrying along the beach road even though she was early.

Gino greeted her with his usual warmth and as he led her in, she noticed in surprise that the restaurant was already nearly full.

She saw with disappointment that 'her' table had already been taken, although the one on the other side was free.

Perhaps when Reno arrived he could ask Gino to put up the dividing barrier so they could have some privacy she thought, although the couple occupying the other table seemed to be totally engrossed in each other and didn't even glance up as she sat down.

Remembering her promise to herself, she offered Gino some money straight away, but he just waived it off saying, "Later, later."

Bringing her drink he didn't stop to chat as usual and she thought he must just be busy with the restaurant being so crowded.

For a while she just watched and listened to the other diners but after a while she realised how long she had been waiting, and glancing at her watch saw it was already gone 10.30.

Starting to get concerned now, she found herself glancing at her watch every five minutes or so as another half hour ticked slowly by.

By quarter past eleven she had decided he wasn't going to show up and she was just preparing to make her escape when the door came crashing open, and she saw the woman she had asked Reno about looking straight at her.

"Why, if it isn't Reno's little friend," she sneered to the crowd behind her, as Jane realised that she was more than a little drunk.

"I hope you're not expecting him," she slurred, "because tonight is party night, so you'll have a long wait."

Before Jane could think of a suitable crushing reply, she had flounced off, bumping into a few tables on the way and nearly knocking a bottle of wine off one of the tables.

Giving her a few minutes so that she wouldn't bump into her again as she left, Jane asked Gino for her bill and to call her a taxi. She didn't feel up to walking the short distance back to her hotel but as she was climbing into it, she saw another taxi passing with the same woman in it and she was sure the man with his arm round her was Reno!

Calling herself every kind of fool for being taken in by his stories, she paid off the cab, collected her key from reception and made a hasty escape to the safety of her anonymous hotel room.

Half angry, half wanting to burst into tears, she got into bed, and tried to sleep.

She was startled by the sound of the phone ringing and wondered who could be calling her at the hotel.

There could be only one person who would have tried to contact her on the hotel switchboard, rather than her mobile, she thought and decided to ignore it.

The phone rang and rang but she remained resolute in ignoring it.

After what seemed an age it stopped and she was just drifting off to sleep when it started ringing again.

She listened to the insistent burr for a while and had just decided to answer and give him a piece of her mind, when it cut off and there was blessed silence.

Chapter 16
Decisions

Jane woke from a fitful night, feeling as if she had hardly slept at all.

Her mind immediately turned to Reno's betrayal of the previous night but deciding that action was better than moping, she determined to revisit 'her' house and start getting her life in order.

She still couldn't believe that with her careful, hesitant, nature, she had spent less than an hour looking at a house and immediately decided to buy it.

Not only that, it was in a country that less than two weeks ago she hardly knew existed. It must be some sort of sunstroke she decided and Reno was just a brief holiday romance.

Someone she could file away in her memory to pull out back in England if a seemingly never-ending winter was making her feel down.

With a start she realised that if she bought the house she wouldn't be facing the snow, rain and cold of an English winter, but would be in a climate that, although it wouldn't be as hot as it was now, nevertheless was likely to be much more clement than she had been used to.

Full of renewed energy, she dressed and went down to breakfast, determining to keep her serious brain fully functional while she weighed up the pros and cons of a possible house purchase in a foreign country.

Catching the hotel shuttle bus as usual, she found herself thinking as she walked towards the villa that might become her new home, that she should have phoned the owners first to ensure it was convenient.

She had no need to worry.

When she hesitatingly knocked on the door, the old man answered and seeing who it was ushered her in immediately, calling out to his wife who emerged from the back room with an equally wide smile.

Stuttering her apologies, she was welcomed wholeheartedly once they were sure she hadn't come to tell them she had changed her mind.

Of course they understood that she wanted to go over 'her' house again.

They would find her a tape measure so she could decide what she wanted to go where. Was she happy with the curtains and blinds that they were leaving behind? If not they could give her the name of someone reliable, and there followed a stream of other information and advice until her head was swimming.

They didn't intend to take much of the furniture with them as their apartment in their daughter's house was fully furnished and they were willing to leave behind anything she thought she might like.

Most of the furniture, although in the older style, was in excellent condition and suited the villa perfectly.

The only things they wanted to keep were their bed, bedroom furniture, some pictures and a few other personal oddments, including some vases and ornaments which had sentimental value for them.

The rest was to be sold off although she had first refusal on anything she wanted for herself.

Jane loved it all but was worried about what the cost would be for such obviously good quality furnishings.

After she had had a good look round and examined what was available, she was astounded at the minuscule price they quoted, which she felt she couldn't possibly accept.

At first they looked rather uncomfortable at her refusal and tentatively remarked that they really didn't think they could let it all go for much less than the price they had said.

Once she had explained she thought she would be robbing them at that price and offered them double, the smiles returned, and after some haggling and insistence on her part, they agreed to meet in the middle and the bargain was sealed.

Even at that price it was still a tremendous bargain, and she knew that she would have had to pay at least five or six times that amount to replace the furniture she had just bought.

What a funny way to do business she thought to herself, the purchaser haggling to increase the offer and having to work hard to get the vendors to accept.

They had come up with all sorts of arguments, that they couldn't be bothered with the hassle of advertising, contacting the local furniture salesman, arranging transportation and dealing with strangers, so she was doing them a favour!

Underlying all their protests she understood that they wanted the furniture to stay with the house and although they were loath to leave their home, it was almost like they had adopted her and were happy that someone they liked would be living in the home they loved, would take good care of it and love it as they had.

They had insisted she stay for lunch with them and she felt quite emotional as she bid them goodbye about 3 o'clock, with promises to come again if not the following day then the day after.

Armed with the directions and address of a local furniture store, with the instructions that she was to be sure to mention she was a good friend of theirs so she wouldn't be ripped off, she found herself outside the shop they had recommended.

Although the entrance was not imposing, she was astounded once inside at the range of styles and variety of the items for sale, with something to suit every taste and price range.

After browsing for a while, and being offered helpful advice by the assistant who was looking after her, she knew that the sleigh style, oak, double bed, complete with mattress and matching large wardrobe and chest of drawers were for her.

Noticing the price, which was not far off what she offered the couple for all the contents but which was still reasonable for such quality, she felt happy with her bargains.

When the manager came to take her order and noticed the address to which they were to be delivered, he mentioned the old couple by name. On being told that she was buying their house he immediately offered her a substantial discount.

It was arranged that he would contact them to sort out a convenient delivery date for after their furniture had been sent on, and she walked out two hours later amazed at how easily everything was taking shape.

Heading back to the hotel, she spent some time phoning and e-mailing to make the necessary arrangements for the deposit to the solicitors, payment to the store for the furniture and a bank transfer to the couple for the goods she was buying from them.

It felt as if she was dreaming as she suddenly realised what she had committed herself to.

All this reminded her that the photos for the notary had been left with Reno. A phone call to the notary's secretary confirmed that yes, the photos had been safely received and Mr Borg was progressing the paperwork.

At least Reno had not let her down in that respect she thought, as she decided she ought to e-mail her sister to update her on the events in her life.

Hardly able to believe herself how much had happened in such a short time she was not surprised to receive a reply from Jena just before she started getting ready for dinner, jokingly asking had she got sunstroke and was she sure she knew what she was doing? At the same time she wished her all the luck in the world and if she was happy to just 'Go for it'.

After all, Jane thought as she read it, Jena had not only upped sticks, moved to a foreign country and bought a house with a man she had only know for a few months, but to a place the other side of the world, a bit different from the three and a half hour flight it would take Jane to get back to London.

Going down to dinner in the hotel, she felt a sense of achievement and satisfaction. Although she was still slightly shocked at what she had committed herself to in the last few days, in her heart she knew the decisions she had made were the right ones.

After a leisurely meal, accompanied by the ubiquitous half bottle of wine, she did something she hadn't done before and went down to the hotel lounge to watch the in-house cabaret.

A brilliant young operatic singer, followed by a comedy duo, helped to keep her mood light and, as she had spent the evening at the hotel and not handed in her key, she had no need to stop at reception.

She was surprised therefore when, as she called goodnight in passing, the young male receptionist called to her by name and leaving his position behind the counter, came running up to her to tell her he had several messages for her.

Glancing through the slips, she realised they were all from Reno, timed at almost hourly intervals since around 10 that morning. The clerk was obviously concerned that they hadn't been given to her when she had collected her key around 6 that evening, and she saw that there had been even more since then, one as recent as an hour ago.

"Would you like me to try the number for you?" the receptionist asked.

"No, thank you," she replied. "But if he phones again, would you be so good as to tell him I have checked out. Thank you very much."

"But," he stuttered, "he would know that's not true."

She realised that as he worked with Reno he probably knew him and she was placing the man in an embarrassing position by asking him to lie for her.

"OK," she said. "Just give him a message. Tell him I will be moving on shortly and please do not try to contact me again."

With that, she turned on her heel and once again escaped to her room.

Chapter 17
Moving on

The following week seemed to fly by.

Apart from several trips to see the notary and sign various papers, she called in to see the old couple frequently and spent some time in both the local shops and the larger stores in nearby towns, to look for various items she would need once she moved into the house.

She was amazed at how her list grew longer every day.

Even though all the furniture had been sorted out, there were so many other things she needed to set up her new home.

Every time she decided on one purchase it reminded her of something else she would need as she was starting from scratch.

She bought a kettle which made her think of cups and crockery, which reminded her of cutlery, which led her to think of condiment sets, and tea cloths and sheets and duvets and bath towels and on and on until her head was spinning and she almost started to panic.

She decided to take a break, and spent two afternoons at the beach just to relax and unwind a bit.

Even then her mind was still whirling but she made the decision that, as she only had herself to worry about, she would concentrate on the necessities and take her time over everything else.

After all, she had all her life before her and she wanted everything exactly right, rather than buying in haste and repenting at leisure.

Finding out about a local market, she returned to the hotel laden down with bedding, kitchen cloths and even dusters, which she surveyed with satisfaction.

Having bought some CDs at the market, the next day was spent in the largest local town, from where she returned tired but happy.

She had found and ordered a home entertainment package. It was complete with music centre, speakers, television and video, which although using the latest technology were in a style which would match the old villa perfectly.

Most of the following day was spent at the villa with the old couple explaining about the electrics and plumbing, showing her the utility meters and leaving her a long list of local tradesmen, who she could contact if she had any problems.

They had introduced her to the young man who serviced the pool once a month and he had readily agreed to continue his regular visits for cleaning and maintenance.

As they were moving out the next morning, they even arranged for the removal men to call at the hotel once they were finished, to collect all her recent purchases and deliver them to the villa for her.

That would just leave her to organise the suitcases she had arrived with, when she checked out of the hotel the following day.

True to their word, the removal men arrived at the hotel about 3 o'clock the next afternoon.

They had even brought with them various boxes and packing cases, for which Jane was sincerely grateful as she was amazed at how much she had accumulated and realised she would never have been able to manage on her own.

They returned about 6 o'clock explaining where they had left everything in the villa and departed well pleased with the payment and large tip Jane had given them.

After a final dinner at the hotel, Jane had arranged with reception to make up her bill ready for her departure early the following morning.

The only sour note was yet another message from Reno, which the clerk handed to her with some trepidation.

She read it, thanked him, and then went to her room where she promptly threw it in the rubbish bin.

That reminded her of yet another thing to add to her list but deciding she would manage with black plastic sacks for the time being, she concentrated on her packing, then made herself a hot drink before retiring to bed for an early night.

Chapter 18
A new beginning

After a restless night, Jane woke very early, ordered room service for breakfast, organised a taxi, paid her bill, and by 8 a.m. had left the hotel for the last time and was driving towards her new home.

After the cab driver had left, she stood for a moment just looking round the villa which seemed eerily empty without the voices of the old couple there to welcome her. Pulling herself together she realised she had a long day ahead of her and putting on her serious head, grabbed her new keys and handbag and set off for the local shops to buy some basic provisions to see her through the day.

Consulting yet another list she returned a short while later with fresh bread, butter, milk, coffee, cheese, ham, salads, fruit and a bottle of her favourite white wine.

Luckily the fridge, humming quietly in the corner of the kitchen, was one of the things she had bought from the previous owners.

Stowing away her provisions, she set to work unpacking the boxes ready to make the place feel more like home.

She was startled by a ring at the doorbell and glancing at her watch saw that it was already 11 o'clock.

Opening the door, she was pleased to see that it was her bedroom furniture being delivered and, once it had been safely installed, was even more pleased to see that it looked perfect in the room, as if it had always belonged there.

Not long after they left, there was another ring at the door, this time for the delivery of her entertainment centre.

Having set it up and tested to ensure everything was working correctly, they too departed and once again the house was silent.

She decided to make herself a light lunch before carrying on and with the sounds of her new CDs playing in the background, sat down to eat it by the pool and enjoy the sunshine.

She could happily have sat there all afternoon but rousing herself after half an hour, went back to sorting out the house.

Jane worked steadily for the rest of the day and with her bed made up and her new possessions stored away in cupboards and drawers, the villa actually felt like home.

There were still her suitcases to be unpacked but feeling hungry, she decided they could wait. After a long, relaxing bath she merely selected what she needed from the opened cases and left them where they were on the bedroom floor.

Feeling too tired to cook and wanting a hot meal after the exertions of the day, she made the decision to treat herself to a meal at Gino's.

After all, she reasoned to herself, she was unlikely to bump into Reno there and anyway, she felt somewhat guilty at neglecting Gino and his wife after promising to visit them.

With everything that had been happening she realised it was ten days or more since she had last been there, and had to make yet another furtive escape from the restaurant.

Just as she was preparing to leave her mobile rang. For a moment she was tempted not to answer it until she realised that Reno didn't have her number.

She was pleasantly surprised to hear the notary's voice, just checking that everything had gone smoothly with the move and to be sure to contact him if she needed anything.

Although she was on her own, she began to appreciate just how many people she had got to know, ready to offer her help or companionship whenever she needed it.

She was now even more convinced that she had made the right decision as she set off in the taxi to renew her acquaintance with Gino and his wife.

After being severely scolded for staying away so long, she enjoyed a pleasant evening and after the rush had died down was joined at her table by Maria and later Gino himself, who hearing the reason for her busy week moving, promised to forgive her neglect only if she told them every single detail of her new home.

They didn't at first mention Reno but surprisingly they did bring up the subject of Paula, the girl who had been in the car with him the last time she had been there, when he had stood her up.

They seemed to want to explain that at heart she was a nice girl, just that she was rather lonely and tried too hard to make friends with the wrong sort of people, who were only interested in her for her money.

Her only true friend was Reno, who was like a big brother looking out for her and rescuing her from difficult situations.

It was a shame that she relied on him so much but he was so good-hearted he would never let her down, even if it interfered with his own personal life.

They made it clear that Paula just needed to find herself a nice young man who cared for her for herself and stop running to Reno every time she was in trouble, or needed some comfort to restore her low self-confidence.

Somewhat surprised at these revelations, she wondered how much Reno had told them about arranging to meet her, or if he had just told them his side of the story so they would make excuses for him.

Finding herself yawning some time later, she realised it was already nearly midnight and, after for once paying her bill in a normal manner, she prepared to leave.

As everyone else had gone and they were preparing to lock up, she told them she would walk the short distance to the corner to pick up a cab to take her home, or even walk as it was such a lovely evening.

Almost as soon as she left the restaurant a car drove past and stopped suddenly a short distance in front of her.

As she got closer the driver's door opened and Paula herself got out.

For a moment Jane was tempted to cross the road to avoid her but calling out her name, Paula pleaded for a few minutes of her time as she had something important to say to her.

Realising for once she was stone cold sober, Jane took a deep breath and sat down on a nearby bench where Paula promptly joined her.

For a moment they sat in silence, then, after a hesitant start, Paula began apologising for the way she had treated Jane and how she had spent the past week trying to find her to explain and ask her forgiveness for her bad behaviour.

Almost in tears, she told Jane that she loved Reno like an older brother, how he had always been protective towards her but this time she had taken advantage of his support once too often.

For the first time ever, he had really ripped into her, told her a few home truths and now was scarcely speaking to her.

She had never seen him so angry. After sulking for a few days, she had taken stock of herself and realised he was right and it was time she grew up and started changing her ways.

She told Jane that even if Reno wouldn't forgive her, she hoped Jane could find it in her heart to understand that it was nothing personal, it was just selfish jealousy. She had been scared that if Reno had someone else he wouldn't be there for her.

Paula said she would understand if Jane never wanted to see or speak to her again but please, would she contact Reno, don't let him suffer because of her stupidity.

Jane was silent for a moment, taking it all in and trying to decide what to believe. Paula offered her a lift home, saying it was the least she could do.

She already knew that she was no longer staying at the hotel and Jane assumed that Reno must also be aware of it.

After telling her the address Paula took some back streets and it only took a few minutes before they were pulling up outside the villa.

"I know this area," Paula told her. "Someone I used to know as a kid lives a few doors away. If you see Frankie while you are staying here, just tell him I said 'Hello'."

"I will," Jane promised, wondering who Frankie was. She half thought of inviting Paula in but it was late and she was tired and with so much to think about, was not really in the mood for company.

"And make sure you phone Reno," Paula called as she drove away.

"But I haven't got his number…" but Paula was already gone.

'Life can sure be full of surprises,' Jane thought to herself as she drank a final coffee sitting by the pool. Twenty minutes later she was in her new bed, fast asleep.

Chapter 19
Life moves on

Despite being in new surroundings and all that had happened the previous day, Jane slept like a log and woke feeling fully refreshed and eager to start the new day.

After finishing her breakfast, a delicious juicy peach and the rest of the bread she had bought the day before, washed down with a cup of coffee, Jane went back upstairs to finish unpacking her suitcases.

She soon had everything put away to her satisfaction, with her toiletries and some of the new towels in her beautiful marble en-suite bathroom.

Notebook and pen in hand, she then took herself on a guided tour of the villa, noting the need to buy some more towels for the second bathroom, and some bedding for the other two bedrooms.

The actual beds and mattresses had been left, so they only needed pillows, pillowcases, sheets and duvets to make them ready for any guests.

'That's if I ever have any,' she thought, so they were not an immediate requirement. Some towels for the downstairs shower room, toilet rolls, a torch and some spare light bulbs were soon added to her list.

In the utility room the washing machine had also been left, together with the iron and an ironing board but she would need to get some washing powder and fabric conditioner.

She had already been up on the roof and seen the washing line but some new pegs would be useful she thought, as, despite the beating sun, there was quite a strong breeze blowing. Perfect drying weather.

She was still undecided as to what to do about Reno. She supposed that if she left a message for him at the hotel it would be passed on, but for the time being she had more important things on her mind, sorting out her new home.

She already had a long list of things to get, which didn't include the basic necessities of stocking her larder.

With all the money she had spent recently she couldn't afford to eat out every night; besides she enjoyed cooking and was looking forward to trying out the cooker and experimenting with the local produce.

Maybe she could do an al fresco dinner party to thank all the people who had supported and helped her along the way.

The old couple whose house she had moved into, the notary and his wife, Gino and Maria, maybe even Mario and his wife to thank them for the hospitality she had enjoyed on their boat.

She even considered Reno and Paula but that was for the future she thought, turning her mind back to the tasks before her.

Wandering through the flower bedecked courtyard, she added a watering can to her list and emerged on the far side of the swimming pool area.

She hadn't previously approached from that direction and noticed for the first time two large wooden structures discreetly tucked away in a corner.

Thinking they might contain some gardening equipment, she rifled through her collection of keys until she found one that fitted and opened the lock.

To her surprise and pleasure the first hut contained a changing area, ideal for the pool, complete with shower unit and stacked in one corner, a dozen sun loungers, together with half a dozen ornate, beautifully carved, small wooden tables and accompanying chairs, complete with cushions.

The other structure was equally a surprise, not containing gardening paraphernalia as she expected but a small, expertly equipped outdoor kitchen, complete with microwave, kettle, barbecue, a small fridge for food and another with racks for holding wine, topped by an ice-making compartment.

There was even a marble food preparation area and a cabinet to hold glasses and crockery, everything necessary for eating near the pool without having to go in and out to the main kitchen in the villa.

Making a note to add more crockery, cutlery, napkins and wine glasses to her list, she couldn't believe how fortunate she had been in finding such a perfect place to live.

She was surprised to hear a ring at the bell as she wasn't expecting any more deliveries.

Obviously the house had been wired up so that visitors could be heard even if the occupants were outside by the pool.

Hurrying back through the house she opened the door to find a stranger, about ten years older than her, standing at the door. The woman explained that she was her neighbour and hearing that she had just moved in, had called round with a cake and a bottle of wine to welcome her to the neighbourhood.

Somewhat overwhelmed at the kindness, Jane invited her in, and sitting over coffee by the pool learned that her name was Gina, her husband Raymond, their grown up son Frankie still lived at home, as well as their younger twin daughters Rita and Rena.

Feeling immediately at ease with the woman and hearing the name Frankie, Jane tentatively asked if the name Paula meant anything to her. "Oh Paula," was the immediate response. "So rich and yet so poor."

At one time she had thought she would be her daughter-in-law but then she had dropped Frankie to run around with older, more sophisticated, men but she didn't think she had found any happiness with them.

She was delighted when Jane relayed her message from Paula to say 'Hello' to Frankie, as he still thought the world of her, even though she had treated him badly. Gina knew he would be over the moon to hear Paula was still thinking of him occasionally.

Before they knew it an hour had passed and Gina took her leave, knowing that Jane must have a million things to do but not before getting her promise that she would join them the following evening, for a barbecue they were holding.

It would give her a chance to meet her other neighbours in an informal atmosphere and if she should see Paula again, to be sure to tell her to come too as she would be very welcome, as would any other friends Jane might want to invite.

Realising that time was passing, Jane grabbed her food shopping list and hit the local supermarket to stock up her larder.

Having to buy all the basics, from salt and pepper, oil and vinegar, kitchen towels, washing up liquid and everything in between, as well as fresh meat, fish, chicken, cheese, potatoes and pasta, her trolley was soon overflowing.

She wondered how she would ever get it all home but the helpful assistant, noticing her dismay and hearing that she was local, said that as it was such a large order, they would be pleased to deliver it about 4 o'clock if that suited her.

Relieved, Jane replied that would be perfect and even added some tinned staples, now that she knew she wouldn't have to try to carry it all.

Leaving the store she realised that although later her cupboards would be full, at the moment she had nothing much left for lunch, so decided to treat herself at the restaurant she had been to before, then head for home.

'Home,' she thought as she unlocked the door and realised that was exactly what it was.

She was surprised to see something in her letterbox and at first assumed it must be just advertising mail as there was no envelope. Opening the note she saw it was from Paula who must have called by while she was out.

Again asking for her forgiveness, she had pleaded for Jane to let her know when she had made it up with Reno and added her own mobile number but not his.

On impulse she sent a text message just saying that she had spoken to Frankie's mother and telling her about the open invitation to the barbecue the following evening if she was interested.

She got an immediate reply saying Paula would be delighted to go and that she would see her there to thank her in person for passing on the message.

The pool looked so inviting after all her shopping that, making a quick decision, she swiftly changed into her tiny bikini and slid into the water.

It was absolutely perfect and she spent the next hour partly swimming and partly just floating in the clear, cool, water, before reluctantly towelling herself off and changing into a cotton robe to await her shopping delivery.

It arrived shortly after 4, and she spent the next hour putting it all away, taking pleasure in the simple tasks of filling the salt and pepper pots and organising what would go where in the kitchen cupboards.

Deciding not to bother to change out of the comfortable towelling robe, she sent an e-mail to her sister to let her know her new address and another to the storage people in the UK, asking them to arrange transportation of her collection of CDs and DVDs to her new address.

Then she set about preparing a lasagne for her supper, which reminded her to add some more cooking pots, pans and oven dishes to her ever growing list of things to buy.

Checking her bank account online, she realised that although she was still well in funds, her savings had been rapidly depleted with all the expenditure over the last few weeks. Making a mental note to visit the bank in the square the next day to arrange to open a local account, she was just going to turn off her computer when an e-mail popped up with an unfamiliar address.

Knowing that she could be opening her computer up to all sorts of junk mail, she was intrigued to know who it was from, but reading it she was glad she had taken the chance.

It was from her old boss, now living in Spain, who apologised for bothering her, and hoped the mail would not just end up in her deleted junk box.

Although he had only been retired a few months and was enjoying his new life, his always active brain was becoming stale and he had started up a small business from his new home.

He had been upset that his sons had sold off the old business and that most of the staff had taken redundancy rather than work for the new company.

He sincerely hoped that she had found new employment but if she hadn't, or if she had a few spare hours a week, he had a proposition to put to her.

Knowing her abilities from having worked so closely together for so many years, he wondered if she would be willing to take on some administrative work for his new company and even look at setting up a small rolling marketing campaign.

Everything could be done on-line, she could do as many or as few hours as suited her and although not as much as her old salary, he would pay her an hourly rate plus any out of pocket expenses.

Excited at the prospect of working with him again, and already deciding that she could do a few hours each morning, say from 9 until 12, or if she had other things to do, she could just as easily spare the time in the late afternoon or evening, she replied immediately saying she would be delighted.

She only just remembered to tell him she was now also living in Europe and gave him her new address and mobile number.

Just as quickly he sent her a reply saying how much he was looking forward to working with her again, that he would phone her the following afternoon to discuss details, arrange the necessary computer access, business phone and so on, with a view to being set up by the end of the month.

Her mind was already turning over possible ideas while she ate her supper, cleared up and spent a short time trying to concentrate on the paperback book she had bought, before she found her eyelids drooping and settled for an early night, ready for another full day ahead.

Chapter 20
Practicalities and surprises

Jane woke early the next morning with the sun shining in her eyes. She realised that as it had been such a beautiful evening she had left the shutters open. Rather than disturbing her, she found herself smiling at this wonderful way of starting a new day.

Her thoughts turned to Mr Baker and she wondered if he was rising to similar sunshine and thinking already about his new business.

She would find out later but meanwhile she had a busy day ahead.

Enjoying her breakfast in her usual spot by the pool reminded her that she should bring out one of the tables and chairs from the storage hut, rather than using a kitchen chair and tray as she had been doing.

'No time like the present,' she thought, as she found the keys, and dragged the furniture out, adding two sun loungers for good measure.

After a quick shower she collected up her passport and other documents and headed out towards the bank.

It was still early but just as she was passing a corner building, the shutters were being opened, and she was given a cheery "Good morning," by a small, wiry, man wearing heavy rimmed glasses.

Returning his greeting she peered inside as she passed, to see row upon row of bookshelves.

Seeing her interest the man beckoned her to come inside and she saw that despite the narrow entrance, the store extended a long way back and must have contained literally thousands of books of all descriptions.

The owner, who introduced himself as Joseph, explained that he was a retired headmaster but all his life books had been his passion.

Finding time hanging heavily on his hands, he had opened his front room as a small bookstore cum library, partly to house his large personal collection of books but also to keep from under his wife's feet, he had told her with a smile.

As more people became aware of his existence and often gave him books they had finished reading, the business had expanded. A year ago he had moved them all to these larger premises to save his house being completely taken over.

For a few cents a day people could borrow the non-fiction and hardback or larger volumes, or actually buy a book from the huge range of paperbacks and hardbacks covering subjects of every description.

Once they had read them, they could return them and get a discount on their next purchase.

It had worked particularly well with tourists, especially the regular visitors, giving them something to read during their stay without the problem of having to pack them to take them home.

The collection was constantly changing and growing as his reputation spread. People often donated books when they were having a clear-out, or needed more room. He had even started a small mail-order business but was struggling with the computer technology which would make it viable.

Surprising herself, Jane offered to help set up the computer side once she was settled; an offer that was readily and gratefully accepted by the beaming proprietor.

Promising to call back next week, Jane reluctantly left the shop and continued to the bank which was now open.

Explaining her requirements, she was shown into a small interview room and joined a few minutes later by a lady who spoke perfect English, with only a very slight accent, who introduced herself as Grace.

As she had her passport, documentation confirming her address and even an ID card which the notary had obtained for her, she was told that, subject to a satisfactory report from her U.K. bankers, there should be no problems at all.

The account was opened there and then, she was given a folder with her new account details and assured that provided her existing bank replied promptly to the e-mail that would be sent that day, she should receive her cheque book, cashcard and euro based credit card within the week.

Pleased with how smoothly things had gone, Jane left the bank realising she would even be able to give Mr Baker details of where to send payments when she spoke to him later that afternoon.

Passing a hardware store with a surprisingly large range of cookware, she found herself selecting item after item of ceramic cooking and serving dishes, saucepans and pots and pans of all description.

Once again she wondered how she would ever manage to get it all home but once again the storeowner came to her rescue.

Although they couldn't deliver as they needed to cover the shop, she was welcome to borrow the shopping trolley and just drop it back when she was next passing.

Nobody she passed seemed the slightest bit surprised at the sight of her pushing the trolley the short distance home. She loved the way her life was made so much easier by being trusted, even though she was a stranger.

Unpacking her purchases, she determined to return the trolley straight away and set off to return to the store.

Expressing her thanks for their help, she was told she shouldn't have bothered to rush straight back and they were pleased to have been able to help.

As she was leaving she noticed the light bulbs and ended up buying not only two packets as spares but also a torch and a small desk fan.

At least this time she could carry her purchases in a couple of carrier bags.

Unlocking her front door once again, she started to put away the previous purchases she had left on the kitchen table but couldn't resist trying out one or two straight away to make herself pasta for lunch.

Washing it down with a glass of chilled white wine, she moved from the poolside table to the lounger, telling herself she would just relax for a minute before clearing up.

She woke with a start half an hour later realising she had dozed off in the midday sun. Getting up she took her lunch dishes into the kitchen and after washing up and putting everything away, she took out her notebook and began crossing off items and reminders that had been bought or completed.

Turning to a fresh page she started jotting down notes of things she wanted to discuss with Mr Baker and had only just finished when her mobile rang.

He was delighted to hear her voice and asked her lots of questions as to how she was enjoying her new life, and what she had been doing since he last saw her.

They then spent half an hour or so discussing the new business, sorting out the mechanics of what she would be doing and how they would communicate developments and cover any problems.

He was pleased that she was able to give him her euro account details for payments and re-iterated that her working hours were totally flexible.

She could work a few hours or a few days one week, then nothing the next, whatever suited her.

He mentioned that he would be able to pay her up to 1200 euros a month without any tax complications, which fitted perfectly with her idea of doing say three hours a day, five days a week.

Pleased with the way things were taking shape he told her he would like to fly over to see her for the day in about two weeks' time, when they could finalise setting up Skype and remote access to be able to launch the business properly shortly after.

Meanwhile she would do some preparatory work, gathering information and setting up databases for the marketing campaign.

When he rang off she found herself excited at the prospect of working again and realised that Joseph, with his experience and knowledge, could be a good source of information.

Deciding a quick swim would be perfect to help her unwind before the evening, she filed away her passport and bank documents before changing and spending an hour relaxing in the pool.

When she emerged from the bathroom, Jane hovered over her wardrobe trying to decide what to wear for her 'meet the neighbours' date that evening at Gina's house. Deciding it would probably be quite informal she selected a sleeveless, knee-length, cotton dress in a turquoise print, with a matching chiffon shawl to cover her shoulders in case it should turn a bit chilly later.

She had no need for tights or stockings as her legs had now tanned a golden brown. As she would only be walking a few yards she added high-heeled open navy sandals. Some light make-up, a dab of perfume and she was ready.

She suddenly felt somewhat shy at meeting all these strangers, but as she was expected between 7.30 and 8 and it was now five minutes to eight, she picked up her evening bag, checked she had her keys and taking a deep breath, walked along to the house.

As she approached she could hear music coming from the back of the house and there was a side gate conveniently open.

Not quite sure of the convention of just letting herself in, she decided to ring the front door bell.

It was opened immediately by a very pretty, bubbly, girl of about sixteen who, with a big smile, said, "Hi, you must be Jane. I'm Rita, come on through, everyone's in the garden."

Passing through the kitchen, she encountered a girl who was the exact image of her companion who, catching her eye, called cheerily, "Hi Jane, I'm Rena. Yes, we're identical twins. Gross isn't it," before sticking out her tongue at her sister then turning back to carry on her conversation with the young lad she had been talking to.

Reaching the garden, Jane saw that it was already crowded with people standing in groups, laughing and chatting or sitting on the various chairs spread around the pool and on the patio.

Gina emerged from the crowd and hurried forward to greet her with a continental kiss on both cheeks before steering her to a long table set up as a bar.

Having got her a drink, she then took her arm to guide her to the smoking barbecue in the far corner and introduced her to her husband Raymond who was controlling the cooking. There were several other men with beers or wine glasses in their hands, who were teasing Raymond and offering their expert advice.

"If you get food poisoning," she said laughingly to Jane, "at least you will recognise him when you face him in court."

Giving her husband an affectionate kiss on the cheek, she then led Jane off to introduce her to some of the other guests, throwing out names and details until Jane's head was reeling.

The atmosphere was so warm and friendly that Jane began thinking if I address any man I meet as Freddie or Joe, and any woman as Maria or Mary, I've got a very good chance of being right.

Refreshing her drink, Gina pointed out another table laden with bowls of pasta and salads, cutlery, napkins and plates and said, "Listen, if you try to be polite here, you will starve to death. Whatever you fancy, just grab it before someone else does. If there is no hot food on the table give your order to the master chef and if he doesn't oblige immediately, tell him he will have me to deal with in the morning! If you want a drink, help yourself, or just rummage in the kitchen until you find what you need."

Laughing, Jane insisted she would be fine as Gina went off to mingle with her other guests.

Taking her at her word, Jane went to help herself to another drink, then found a chair to sit down for a few minutes and enjoy the party atmosphere.

She was joined on and off by a constant stream of people coming to say "Hello," and welcoming her to their neighbourhood.

Almost every encounter ended in an invitation to join them for lunch, dinner, or coffee any time she was free and she began to feel that she would need to live here for years to accept and reciprocate the hospitality.

Starting to feel hungry Jane made her way to the food table and helped herself to a heaped plate from the various foods available, including, she thought to herself with a smile, ample hot food so Raymond would not be in the dog house.

As she was returning to her table she caught sight of an older male version of the twins, engrossed in the company of a woman who looked familiar.

Although she couldn't properly identify her, as the man who she assumed must be Frankie, was blocking her view.

As she got back to her seat she heard her name being called and looking up, found a beaming Paula standing in front of her next to an equally smiling Frankie.

"Jane," Paula said. "It's so good to see you again. Can I introduce you to my very special friend Frankie?"

Taking her hand Frankie said, "I'm so pleased to meet you Jane. Thank you so much for passing on Paula's message and persuading her to come tonight. I'm really grateful."

Jane started to protest that she hadn't done anything but was interrupted by Paula's thanks as well. She felt that nothing more need to be said as the couple walked off with Frankie's arm round Paula's waist and their eyes only for each other.

Gazing after them she didn't see Gina approach until she sat down in the chair next to her.

"Are you OK? Can I get you anything," Gina asked, then without waiting for a reply, looked at the departing couple and said, "Maybe I will get my daughter-in-law after all."

They sat chatting for a few minutes, then after being reassured that Jane had everything she wanted and was enjoying herself, Gina once again left her to check on her other guests.

As the evening progressed, feeling well fed, totally at ease and with more than a few glasses of wine inside her, Jane was relaxing, enjoying the background buzz of conversation and watching people dancing to the music from the stereo, when a shadow loomed over her.

Expecting one of the many guests who had taken pains to ensure she was not left on her own for too long, she found herself looking up into the deep brown eyes of Reno.

"May I join you?" he asked in the deep voice that sent her whole body quivering. "I think we need to talk."

Before she could stutter a reply, he had sat on the vacant seat next to her, which he pulled closer until they were almost touching.

He started by telling her not to interrupt, just to let him talk first, then he would accept whatever she said once he had finished his explanation.

He started off by telling her a lot of what she had already gathered, how he had known Paula since she was a child, how he loved her like a kid sister, how she had changed from a loving sweet girl to a hard-nosed bitch when she had too much to drink and got in with the wrong crowd.

He explained how underneath she was a lonely frightened girl still, not the sophisticated lady she tried to pretend she was.

He told Jane he had been so looking forward to meeting her at Gino's when he had come across Paula, almost paralytic, stumbling in the gutter and had to call a taxi to get her home.

She was in such a bad state that no way could he leave her like that, God knows what would have happened to her.

He had rushed back to Gino's but she had already left. He had tried to phone her at the hotel but his calls went unanswered and he assumed she had written him off and gone out with other friends.

He had left messages at the hotel but she was never available, and never returned his calls. Then she checked out of the hotel and he thought she was just not interested and wanted to avoid him.

He thought she must have someone else and was trying to just move on but she kept coming into his thoughts. He couldn't forget her and had been a grumpy, miserable, old bear for the last week or so. Eventually even his best friends had said he must see her again, whatever it took, to find out once and for all, as he had changed so much.

That was it, he had said everything he had to say, except that he really wanted to see her again and get to know her better, but it was up to her where they went from here.

He had just finished speaking but before she could answer, Paula appeared beside them with her arms still wrapped around Frankie. Giving them both a big kiss she said to Reno, "Do you realise what a lovely woman you have? Make sure you care for Jane as you have always cared for me, or else!"

Still engrossed in each other Paula and Frankie left them as Reno stared in amazement. "What was that all about?" he asked. "How does she know you?"

As this was easier to answer than his previous question Jane explained how Paula had sought her out to explain what Reno himself had just told her. Jane had to confess how, unwittingly, she had been instrumental in getting Paula and Frankie back together again.

"You are really something," he said as he leant over to kiss her cheek.

As she turned her head to protest she had not really done anything, they ended up with their faces inches apart and it was the most natural thing in the world for their lips to meet.

The kiss started as slow and sweet but gradually deepened until they were in a warm and passionate embrace, until Jane's head was reeling and all she could think of was pulling him closer and closer, so he would melt into her and the two become one.

When they eventually came up for air, both had dazed expressions on their faces and for a moment neither could speak.

"Wow," Reno eventually whispered. "Does that mean you have forgiven me?"

"Not yet," Jane smiled. "I need a few more of those to convince me."

As Reno came closer to repeat the performance, she laughingly pushed him away, saying what sort of person would her new neighbours think had moved into the area.

At his puzzled look she had to explain that she was living in the villa, how she had met Gina and the reason for her being there that night.

It occurred to her to ask what Reno was doing there. He explained that Paula had insisted he came, saying she had something very important to tell him.

He had thought of not bothering, as he was still so upset with her and it was only at the last moment he had changed his mind.

He was even more surprised when he had sought out Paula but apart from saying 'Hi' and giving him a quick kiss on the cheek, she had turned back to Frankie and not bothered to try to explain.

It was only when he had noticed Jane sitting alone that he had turned to Paula and smiled his understanding.

She had blown him a quick kiss and mouthed "Go for it," before turning again to Frankie with a big grin on her face. Maybe she had grown up at last.

Jane still felt like she was in a dream but remembering where she was, needed to get things on a less romantic footing.

She started telling Reno about the events of her recent life. Her enthusiasm bubbled though as she described her old boss, his recent offer and how excited she was at the prospect of assisting him in his new business.

When it came to describing her new home she felt a bit reticent about telling him she intended to buy it, so she just intimated how lucky she had been to find such a perfect place to rent at such a reasonable price.

It was obvious how much she loved the place and her pleasure showed when she was talking about the simple things like buying pots and pans and how convenient the local stores were for the small necessities like light bulbs.

She realised she was babbling but he just gave her that wry smile, without comment.

At that point they were joined again by Gina, who raising her eyebrows at how close they were sitting but not passing any comment, just said she gathered you two had met and hoped they had enjoyed the evening.

Realising it was getting late, Jane said it had been wonderful. She was really appreciative of the hospitality she had been shown and she would try to reciprocate as soon as she could.

A lot of people had already left so Jane again thanked her hostess and said she would be going home now, at which Reno immediately told Gina that he would escort her.

With a knowing smile, Gina thanked them for coming and bade them goodnight.

Somewhat embarrassed, Jane again expressed her thanks for the evening and stood up to leave, half-heartedly protesting to Reno that it was only a few yards away and she would be fine.

"Don't worry," he said with a smile. "Once I've seen you to your front door I'll leave and go home."

Adding his thanks to Gina for her hospitality, he turned to look for Paula but she was sitting on Frankie's lap, with her eyes gazing into his and as they were talking quietly together they didn't even notice his going.

Taking Jane's hand he led her out the back way and walked the few yards with her to the villa, then stood quietly as she fumbled for her key to the front door.

Taking it from her he held the door open while she went inside, pushing it half closed behind him, took her in his arms, and gave her a long, gentle kiss.

Before she could get her thoughts together, he merely smiled, whispered "Goodnight," and left, closing the door behind him.

Unsure whether to be pleased or disappointed, she went through into the kitchen, made herself a hot drink, and took herself off to bed.

Chapter 21
A perfect day

After all that had happened the previous day, Jane hadn't expected to sleep well but she woke quite late, feeling rested and with a smile on her face.

Eating her breakfast by the pool, she suddenly heard her mobile ringing.

Picking it up, she half expected it to be Mr Baker so was surprised to hear a deep, now familiar, voice say, "Good morning. Have you any plans for the day?"

"Er, not really. Where are you?" she stuttered, then felt all kinds of a fool for asking such a stupid question.

"Outside your front door," came the laughing reply and phone still in hand, she went to open it for him.

He stood on the doorstep with a big smile on his face, looking casual but devastating as always. It was only when he put his phone back in his pocket that she remembered to turn hers off.

Following her through to the patio he noticed her unfinished breakfast and, urging her to finish it before it got cold, helped himself to a cup of coffee then sat down to join her.

"The chariot is outside the door and the chauffeur is at your disposal for the day," he said. "So your wish is my command. What would you like to do?"

"I had intended to look for some more bed linen but it's not important, it can wait," Jane replied. "So anything you like, really."

"Great," he smiled. "You get ready while I wash these up and we'll be off. Don't bother to change on my account, you look beautiful like that."

Embarrassed, she looked down at the short cotton shift she had slipped on to eat breakfast and realised she hadn't even brushed her hair properly.

"I'll only be a minute," she called as she dashed to her bedroom to get dressed properly and make herself respectable.

Five minutes later she came back suitably attired, to find the breakfast things cleared away and him reclining on one of the loungers, with his eyes hooded against the morning sun.

For a moment she just stood looking at him unobserved. She noticed his muscles under the sleeveless T-shirt he was wearing and his tanned legs and thighs under the smart linen shorts.

'Wow' she thought. 'He is really fit – in all senses of the word,' then blushed when she found he had opened his eyes and was watching her.

"I'm ready," was all she could think to say as he stood up and led her to the open topped jeep parked outside.

Jane loved the feeling of total freedom, with the wind blowing through her hair as Reno expertly drove the jeep along the coast road until they were in an area she hadn't been to before.

They didn't talk much but now and again she would catch Reno glancing sideways at her. He was smiling when he saw the look of pure joy on her face, as, with her head leant back against the seat, she raised her face to the sun steaming through the open roof.

After a while he took a side road leading away from the sun, turned a few corners, then parked the jeep in an open car park.

"Where are we?" she asked. He told her the name of the village, which she intended to look up on a map when she got back, but had no idea how to spell.

Taking her hand, he led her through some other side streets until they came to an open square with the sea bordering one side and the other filled with market stalls selling goods of every description.

Although it looked chaotic, she realised one side was dedicated to livestock and food, everything from birds in cages to live chickens, newly caught fish, crabs and enormous prawns, home baked bread, cakes and freshly picked fruit and vegetables.

Along another section were antique fire tongs and buckets, carved wooden ornaments, glassware, both practical and ornate, ceramic dishes, cooking pots, gardening planters and flower troughs.

Another aisle led to tourist goods, bric-a-brac and everything from sunglasses and CDs to ornaments, decorative plates and wall plaques.

The final section covered clothing, fabrics and textiles: jeans, T-shirts, dresses, lengths of cloth in all colours and designs, leather and suede jackets, handbags, lace tablecloths, beautifully made baby clothes and finally towels, sheets and pillow cases.

"You mentioned you needed some more bedding," he said and she was amazed and pleased that he had remembered the chance remark from their previous conversation.

She browsed happily for a while with Reno's arm slung casually round her shoulder. Before too long she had another huge pile of parcels tied up with string, together with various bags filled to overflowing with bed linen.

While she had been deciding, Reno had been chatting with the old woman in their own language and from the cackles of laughter and beaming smiles she was giving him, guessed he had been flirting outrageously.

As they turned to leave, the old lady blew him a toothless kiss, then called out something which made him laugh out loud.

Blowing the old lady a kiss in return, he said in English, "We will," and still smiling but now laden down with all her shopping, he led Jane away.

"What did she say?" Jane couldn't resist asking.

"She said they are lucky sheets, blessed by God," he replied. "She insisted we come back soon when we needed the cot sheets for the beautiful babies we would be having."

With no idea how to reply, Jane heard him suggesting that while he took the parcels back to the car, she carry on browsing for a while.

If she followed the central aisle to the end she would find an open-air café area where he would meet her in about twenty minutes.

Taking advantage of him having his arms full, she kissed him lightly on the cheek and teased that he only wanted to get rid of her to go back and chat up his new girlfriend! Laughing again he started making his way back to the car while she turned and walked back to one of the other sections.

Earlier she had noticed a stall with some beautiful turquoise long drop earrings but when she had tried to stop, Reno had said they could come back later and urged her on.

After looking around for a while, she was sure she had found the right place but couldn't see the earrings.

Asking the stall owner, he told her that he knew the ones she meant but they had been sold not five minutes ago.

Although he tried to tempt her with some other beautiful items, Jane turned away disappointed as those where the ones she had set her heart on.

She spent a while longer looking at the other goods, then, realising time was passing, headed towards the central aisle Reno had pointed out.

After a few minutes following the path which sloped steadily upwards, she found herself in a large open area with flower beds, small circular ponds, some with fountains above them, benches scattered at intervals, mostly under the shade of overhanging trees and at the far side, a long stone coloured wall overlooking the sea. She noticed Reno immediately, sitting on a chair in front of a wrought iron table by a small kiosk with a brightly coloured roof.

Watching him unobserved for a moment, she couldn't help seeing how nearly all the passing females gave him a second admiring look; the older ones and those with male companions surreptitiously, the younger, single ones quite blatantly.

Noticing her approach, he stood up, kissed her lightly on the cheek and indicated the two tall glasses of fresh orange juice in front of him.

"I thought you would be ready for a drink after all that hard work shopping," he smiled.

Taking the chair next to him, she raised the glass and downed half of it in one go as she realised how thirsty she was.

She was happy to just sit, resting and watching the world go by for a while, then he led her over to the wall and they stood gazing out to sea as he pointed out the small uninhabited islands in the distance.

"Do you like boats?" he asked suddenly.

Hearing that she did, he glanced at his watch, said "Come on," and taking her hand led her towards a gap in the wall, with steep stone steps sloping down to the sea below. She found herself in a small harbour area and, hurrying her along the walkway, he helped her along the gangplank onto a boat, just as it was preparing to leave.

Following him to the upper deck they settled themselves breathlessly onto a bench at the side. Leaning on the railing she watched as the boat reversed out of the berth and turning, headed out to the open sea in the direction of the islands he had pointed out from above.

With the breeze blowing through her hair, the sun on her face, the lap of the water below and the perfect companion besides her, Jane felt as if she could have stayed there forever.

After a while Reno got up and saying he wouldn't be long, disappeared down the steps to the lower deck.

Closing her eyes she let her mind drift until feeling a shadow passing over her, she opened them again to see Reno standing over her with a large square cool bag in one hand. "Lunch," he said, then sat down beside her again as the boat approached one of the islands and turned to reverse into a mooring.

Once they had docked, he took her hand to lead her along the gangplank and then up a steep path leading away from the sea.

At first the sides of the path were rocky and open and he pointed out to her the bright coloured flowers hidden between the boulders and the tiny lizards scuttling for cover as they approached.

As they went further, the landscape changed to include more brush and bushes and eventually grassland, with trees providing cover from the heat of the sun.

Walking mainly in peaceful silence, now and again he would point out various small animals carrying on their lives in the wooded undergrowth, or birds building their nests in the branches of the trees above.

He obviously knew the island well as, leading her through a half hidden bower of overhanging trees, they emerged to a grassy knoll on the top of the cliff, with a small stream cascading into a waterfall to the sparking blue sea way below.

Setting down the box, he opened it to reveal plastic cups and glasses, cutlery, napkins and plates.

As he removed the cardboard divider she saw nestling underneath two bottles of water, some fresh filled baguettes, cheese, large juicy red tomatoes and even two small bottles of wine.

Pouring them both a glass from one of the bottles, he wedged the other between some rocks in the flowing stream to keep cool.

Dipping her fingers into the water she was surprised to feel how cold it was but so refreshing after the heat of the sun and their exertion in climbing up to this secluded spot.

All she could hear around her were the singing of the birds, the occasional rustle of the undergrowth and the distant splash of the stream as it hit the sea.

The fresh air had given her an appetite and she tucked into the delicious food with relish, washing it down with sips of the refreshing light white wine.

When they had finished, she rinsed her hands in the stream then lay back against the trunk of the tree with Reno sitting close enough to touch.

"Tell me about yourself," she said quietly. At first he didn't answer, then he told her he had been born on the island.

His father had been a skilled general handyman and as a young boy he had learnt from him all the basics of carpentry, plumbing, electrical work, general building, and even stonemasonry.

He was the eldest of five, two brothers and two sisters. One sister now lived in Canada, one brother in Australia, the others still lived on the island, as did his parents and he had more nieces and nephews than he could keep track of, with another one on the way shortly.

He loved to travel and had spent some time working in various hotels all over the world, until he had come back to the island about two years ago.

"What about girlfriends? Did you never want to settle down and get married?" she found the nerve to ask.

"I did have one or two short term relationships," he replied honestly. "But then I got the wanderlust again and moved on. What about you, why did you never marry?" he asked, turning the conversation back to her.

Thinking about it, she didn't really know the answer.

"I suppose I just never found the right man," she eventually replied. "I enjoyed the challenges of my job, had the company of my sister and although I had one or two boyfriends, they never really felt right. I guess I just drifted until I was made redundant and decided to start controlling my life, instead of just letting it control me."

"Do you think you made the right decision in coming here?" he asked.

"Definitely," she whispered, as he moved closer and taking her in his arms, drew her into his sweet kiss.

A long time later they came up for air and then she nestled closer into him. They sat for a while in silence with her head on his shoulder, both thinking their own thoughts.

"I hate to say it," he said eventually, "but we need to start heading back to catch the boat soon."

Reluctantly, she stood up, and after packing up the picnic things, they walked hand in hand back the way they had come until they reached the boat.

All too soon they arrived back at their joining point and he led her a different way back, up a less steep road, until they arrived at the jeep for the drive home.

When they got there, he came in to carry her purchases from the market but then, telling her he would pick her up for dinner about eight the following evening, with a quick kiss, he was gone.

For a moment she felt lost, then pulling herself together, she took her parcels upstairs ready to pack away.

Determined not to spend the evening just mooning about, she started preparing her evening meal, then, while it was cooking, opened up her laptop and started setting up the databases she had discussed with Mr Baker, was it really only the day before?

It felt like a lifetime ago.

She worked steadily for a while until the enticing aromas coming from the kitchen made her realise her dinner was nearly ready.

It was only as she sat down to eat it that she let her mind drift back over the day and she wasn't even aware of the smile hovering over her face, as she relived every minute of her perfect day.

Suddenly she realised there had never been any mention of seeing her during the day, or even that evening and she wondered what he would be doing. 'Working of course, you fool,' she reprimanded herself and maybe catching up on some sleep, or all the other chores normal people have to do.

It was just as well she had accepted Mr Baker's offer she thought, otherwise she might have found herself turning into one of those bored, spoilt, women with too much time on their hands, who never considered anyone but themselves.

After clearing up, she went back to do some more work for an hour or so, before closing her laptop with a yawn and taking herself off to bed.

Chapter 22
Setting a routine

Waking with a smile from pleasant half-remembered dreams, Jane decided it was about time she tackled some housework.

Although it was warm the sun was trying to hide behind some clouds this morning, which was just as well she thought, as it gave her the incentive to get on instead of lounging around the pool.

Putting on an old cotton dress, she clipped her hair back and realised how much it had grown since that day in London with the make-over that had been the start of her new life.

She noticed too that some darker roots had started to show through; time to find a hairdresser she thought.

A few hours later, feeling decidedly grubby, but with the house gleaming once again and even some sheets blowing on the line, she felt satisfied with her morning's work. On impulse she had decided to strip her bed and put on the new 'lucky' sheets she had bought yesterday; a thought which made her think of Reno, as most things did these days.

Looking forward to the evening she wondered where he would take her and once again, whether she should offer to pay or split the bill.

She had wondered what the wages were like here. Although things seemed very cheap compared to London prices, she assumed that incomes were also a great deal lower.

Having a quick wash to get rid of the worst of the grime, she set about making her lunch, which she ate sitting on the patio rather than by the pool as usual, although the sun was now trying to break through.

Washing the floor earlier, she had noticed a row of electrical sockets. After clearing up after her meal, she plugged in her laptop to charge the battery and settled down to a few hours' work.

Engrossed in her new interest, she glanced at her watch to see it was already getting on for 5 o'clock.

Stretching to relieve her cramped muscles, she shut down her computer then went up to the roof to bring down the washing which was already dry.

Making herself a hot drink, she sat down in a comfortable armchair in the living room and put on the radio as background music while she relaxed for five minutes.

Nearly an hour later she woke with a start to realise she had gone right off to sleep. I'm definitely getting lazy, she thought, adding, 'find out about the gym' to 'find a hairdressers' on her 'to do' list for the following day.

After a long soak in the bath, she put out the dress and underwear she intended to wear later, then spent some time trying to restyle her hair into a semblance of its original sophisticated style.

As it was still early she sat for a while in the armchair but was sure this time she would not fall asleep as she was too excited at the prospect of seeing Reno again.

She was just putting the finishing touches and trying to decide which earrings to wear, when she heard his ring at the bell, just before eight.

He looked gorgeous as always and she noticed that he was slightly more formally dressed than she had seen him before, even to having a smart jacket slung casually over his shoulder.

"I won't be a minute," she said as she invited him in.

Turning as they reached the lounge, she found him right behind her as he pushed aside her hair and gently kissed her neck.

"You smell nice," he said. "But you've forgotten your earrings."

"I was just putting them on," she started to say, then stared in amazement at the small box he was holding out to her, containing the earrings she had so admired in the market.

"But he told me he had sold them," she stuttered as she put them on.

"I know," he smiled. "I saw you coming back for them and you nearly caught me. I meant to give them to you yesterday but I put them in the glove compartment when I took the parcels back to the car and with everything else happening, I forgot all about them until this morning."

They looked perfect and she was overwhelmed, not only at the gift but the fact he had noticed how much she liked them and taken the trouble to go back to get them for her.

Leaning forward to give him a light thank you kiss, she found herself wrapped in his arms with the kiss getting more passionate by the minute.

Pulling apart, he gazed at her with his smouldering, dark, eyes and told her that they had better get going before he forgot himself completely and totally ruined her make-up.

Taking her hand they went out and she noticed a sleek, modern car parked outside.

To her surprise, as she had expected the jeep, he helped her into it and settled her into the soft black leather seats.

"Have you got a car for every day of the week?" she teased.

He hesitated for a moment before replying, "Not exactly, they belong to the hotel and I can just borrow one when I need it. Most of the time I use my motorbike."

Despite their long conversations yesterday, when she had started to find out more about him, he still had the air of a man of mystery which only added to his more obvious attributes.

After driving for about fifteen minutes he pulled into the entrance of a beautiful hotel, similar to the one she had stayed in, that looked as if it had been converted from an ancient manor house.

He was greeted with great respect, as someone came to park the car and they were led through a vine-bedecked courtyard into an open area with fairy lights twinkling amongst the trees.

The soft glow of candles on the tables, mixed with the heady aroma from the shrubs and flowers in hanging baskets, gave it a very romantic atmosphere. They were shown to a secluded table surrounded with trees on three sides, which added to its privacy.

"This is beautiful," she smiled, "but it looks expensive," she added as she glanced at the menus they had been handed.

Again that slight hesitancy before he replied, "Don't worry, I get a discount," and brushed away her offer to split the bill, saying "You can treat me to a wildly exotic meal another time – like a burger on the beach! I might even push the boat out and get you to buy me a fruit juice as well, so you had better start saving."

Laughing, she gave in and turned back to look through the distressed ornate leather menu with its embossed logo which looked like an ancient coat of arms.

"Is there anything you don't like?" he asked her as he pointed out various specialities on the menu.

"Not really," she replied. "I'm not keen on eggs, but apart from that I like to try out things I haven't tasted before. I'm quite experimental in my tastes; actually I just love food," she laughed, feeling a little embarrassed.

"Good," was his only response. "I do like a woman to look like a woman, not a stick insect," making her feel better.

That got them to talking about keeping fit and exercise and he told her that the gym in the hotel near her villa was excellent and he was a member there himself.

"What else do you like doing?" she asked.

"Reading," he replied. "Swimming, nature and talking to beautiful women. What about you?"

"The same," she replied, feeling her cheeks going pink. "Except make it beautiful men not women," then blushed even more at her trite response.

Hearing his deep laugh, she realised he was teasing her again. It was only later it struck her how skilfully he always turned the conversation away from himself whenever he was asked personal questions.

The meal was excellent and she had particularly enjoyed the mixed seafood starter, which, he told her, included tiny local sea urchins, sautéed in butter, garlic and herbs. "Do you cook?" she asked and again that slight hesitation before he told her he could if he had to but mainly he had his meals at the hotel.

She was just going to ask him more about the work he did, when he took her hand and invited her to dance to the band that had been playing quietly in the background.

He was a good dancer and, enjoying the intimacy as he guided her around the dance floor, she soon forgot her questioning.

It was only as they were returning to their table that she was reminded of it, when he was hailed by a group of smart suited businessmen seated at a table near the centre of the room.

Excusing himself for a moment, he went over to have a quick word with them, making no attempt to take her with him to introduce her.

It struck her as odd that an ordinary workman should be greeted so cordially by what were obviously wealthy and influential people, especially when, as he returned to take her back to their secluded table, she thought she heard the words, "Boardroom, tomorrow."

As they returned to their seats he offered no explanation as to who they might have been, merely recommending the home-made coconut ice cream to go with the exotic fruit pastry dessert.

Finishing off their second bottle of wine and with a liqueur to accompany their coffee, she did wonder about drink driving limits.

Sometime later they got up to dance again and she noticed the businessmen leaving, but, with a quick wave, Reno had led her to the far side of the dance floor and concentrated all his attention on her.

After a session of more upbeat music, the band reverted to a slower, more romantic, mood once again, before saying goodnight, and beginning to pack up their instruments.

Glancing at her watch, she was surprised to see it was already gone 1 o'clock and most of the patrons had already left the restaurant.

Excusing himself, Reno stood up and she watched him walk over to the maître d' and stand chatting to him for a few minutes.

It was only as he laid a few notes on the table as a tip, that she realised she hadn't seen him take out his wallet, or pay a bill, while he had been talking.

"Ready?" he asked, as he led her outside and into a waiting cab.

She wondered about the car he had driven her there in, then remembered his telling her about the fleet of hotel cars and assumed he had just been returning it.

At least she had no worries about his driving under the influence, she thought as she settled back into his arms for the drive home.

When they reached the villa he left her to open the door while he spoke to the driver, who then drove off.

Again she hadn't seen any money change hands but perhaps he had paid while her back was turned she thought. As the flat he had taken her to previously was only just around the corner he could easily walk home from her place.

"Coffee?" she asked as he settled himself onto the large settee in the lounge.

"Please," he replied, then pulled her onto his lap when she returned with the tray.

The coffee was soon forgotten as he kissed her and his caresses became more and more intimate.

Slipping off her dress, his hands traced the outline of her breasts over her lacy bra and soon even that barrier disappeared, as he bent his head to take her swollen nipples into his mouth.

Feeling the warmth flowing through her, she felt she would explode as he continued his exploration of her body, whispering into her ear and kissing her neck in between returning his attention to her breasts.

When he stood up she felt her legs turn to jelly and, without his supporting arm, she didn't think she could have climbed the stairs as he led her into her bedroom.

Excusing herself she left him as she fled to the bathroom and quickly taking off her make-up, splashed her face with cold water to cool her overheated blood.

She heard him using the other bathroom and when she returned to the bedroom he was sitting on the bed, clad only in a pair of dark underpants.

As he stood up, she couldn't help her eyes glancing at the bulge between his muscular thighs, showing he was as excited as she was.

Her breath came out in a gasp as he took off his last article of clothing and his magnificent male member sprung to attention.

Leading her to the bed, he pushed back the 'lucky' sheets, gently removed her underwear and continued the seduction he had begun downstairs.

When she thought she could take no more pleasure, he moved himself on top of her and for a moment she felt a surge of panic at the size of him, especially as it had been so long since she had had a physical relationship.

She needn't have worried. Sensing her fear he used his arms to support himself while his tongue continued its magic, until eventually it was she who pulled him into her to satisfy the sweet torment that had built up.

Slowly they settled into a rhythm together which built up until she exploded into wave after wave of ecstasy, followed a few seconds later by Reno taking his own release.

"Wow," was all he said as he rolled off her and then gathered her into the harbour of his arms while they got their breath back.

When he got out of bed she felt totally bereft until he returned a few minutes later with some glasses of water, which she gulped thirstily.

As she turned to put the glass on her bedside table, her breast brushed his arm and before she knew it they were having a repeat performance.

It was even better this time, if that was possible, as gaining confidence, she initiated some moves of her own which left him struggling to retain his control, until they peaked simultaneously, and collapsed exhausted.

Totally satiated Jane drifted off to sleep, safe in the comfort of his arms and feeling this was where she had always belonged.

She partly roused some time later, feeling something was missing and, opening her eyes, saw Reno already dressed and preparing to leave.

Sensing she was awake, he turned back to the bed and tenderly kissing her lips, whispered "Sleep."

The next minute she heard the door closing softly and he was gone.

Catching sight of the bedside clock she saw it was nearly 4 o'clock and the darkness of the night was starting to give way to a breaking dawn.

Chapter 23
The morning after

Jane slept late the following morning and it was already gone nine when she stretched and got out of bed.

Feeling her muscles ache, she had remembered the activity of the night before and wondered what Reno was doing.

After taking a warm, soothing, bath she got dressed and went down to the lounge where her attention was caught by the coffee cups sitting where they had left them on the low table, their contents now cold and congealed.

Smiling to herself as she remembered the reason they hadn't been cleared away last night, she washed up and prepared herself some breakfast.

Noticing she needed some more bread, she thought she would spend the morning sorting out about the gym and hairdresser's once she had been to the baker's.

Straightening the settee cushions just as she was leaving, she heard a jangling sound, and digging down the back came up with a bunch of keys.

'Reno must have dropped them last night,' she thought, then wondered how he had managed to let himself in if one was his front door key.

Putting them in her handbag, she walked down to the square, and seeing a hairdresser's up a side road went in and made herself an appointment for later than morning.

Passing the hotel she enquired at reception and was directed to the adjoining door at the side which led to the gym.

It looked bright, modern and well equipped and glancing round in the vague hope of seeing Reno, she noticed that the clientele was a mixture of hotel guests and locals, both male and female.

Their ages ranged from some young, fit looking, boys to a few ladies many years her senior.

Feeling it would suit her well, she completed the application form and deciding to pay the annual membership rather than the daily rate, left with her new plastic membership card safely tucked into her purse.

After buying some more bread and a couple of succulent pasties for lunch, she realised she still had some time to kill before her hairdresser's appointment.

Remembering the keys, she took a chance on finding him in and made her way to the flat where Reno lived.

The outer door was locked but trying one of the keys it opened easily and she found herself climbing the steps to the apartment she remembered on the first floor.

Unsure what to do next she knocked on the door, which was quickly opened by a pretty woman with a toddler hanging on one hip.

Taken back Jane stuttered, "I'm sorry to bother you I was looking for Reno. I think I must have got the wrong flat."

Glancing at her watch, the woman said, "He should be here soon, why don't you come in and wait."

"I don't want to disturb you," Jane said. "I just found these keys and thought they belonged here."

Taking them from her the woman smiled, "That man of mine would lose his head if it wasn't attached to his neck. Thank you so much for returning them."

At that moment a young voice called out from the kitchen, "Daddy home, Daddy feed me."

Turning to the voice the woman called out, "Finish your lunch darling, Daddy be home soon."

Taking advantage of the distraction Jane called goodbye and fled down the steps and back onto the street before the woman could ask her any more questions.

Half upset, half angry, both with herself for being taken in and with Reno for taking advantage of her and blatantly lying to her about his family life, she found herself in a small children's playground, where she took comfort in food.

Opening the bags she had bought at the bakers she devoured her lunch, then, noticing the time, made her way to her hairdresser's appointment.

Despite the protests, she decided to go back to her natural colour, although the sun had already bleached it from mousy brown to a soft honey.

She was pleased with the results, which with a few highlights gave her a cross between the dyed London blonde and a more natural, although not dowdy, soft brown, closer to her original colour.

Not wanting to be available should Reno try to contact her but unsure how she could avoid him, she noticed a flyer in her letter box offering overnight trips to a neighbouring island which seemed to offer the perfect solution.

Phoning the number, she was pleased to hear they had a vacancy for the trip that very evening. Hastily throwing together an overnight bag, she was ready and waiting when the minibus called to pick her up at 5.30 that evening.

After a short drive to the ferry, she was met on the other side by another minibus which drove for a while through green pastures before arriving at a country hotel which was to be her refuge for the night.

After checking in, and being shown to her small but scrupulously clean single room, she browsed the tour itinerary which included welcoming cocktails at eight, followed by a buffet dinner and traditional floorshow.

After showering and changing, she made her way down to the foyer for an introductory welcome party where she was introduced to her fellow guests.

An Englishman in his forties, introducing himself as Steve, made an immediate beeline for her. When they were led through to the dining area, she was not surprised when he commandeered the seat next to her and made it his duty to look after her for the night.

Although she didn't fancy him, he was pleasant company and she found his open admiration and lack of guile a welcome change from the heavy intricacies of her recent relationship with Reno.

He made sure her wine glass was topped up, that she had everything she wanted with her meal and held her closely, but without passion, when they got up to dance later in the evening.

Seeing her to her bedroom door later that evening, he accepted her refusal to let him in for a nightcap without taking offence and with a chaste goodnight kiss, just said he looked forward to seeing her in the morning.

Despite everything she slept well. Going down to breakfast the next morning she was not surprised to find that Steve had saved her a place next to him.

She spent the day in his company on the sightseeing coach tours that followed and was impressed by the information he was able to give her about the various sights, as he had obviously genned up on each place they visited.

She was quite sorry to see him go when they finally returned to take the last ferry back that evening, and were eventually dropped home to their various destinations by minibus shortly before midnight.

Exhausted and pleased that she had been able to keep Reno out of her thoughts for at least most of the last twenty-four hours, she got into bed and finally managed to sleep.

Chapter 24
Revelations

Waking late after a disturbed night, Jane had only just finished dressing when she heard the doorbell ring.

Bracing herself for a confrontation, she was not sure if she was pleased or disappointed to find it was only a messenger, delivering her CDs which had been shipped from storage in London.

After finishing her breakfast and spending a couple of hours on her computer, she decided it was time she started her keep fit regime. Changing into casual T-shirt and joggers, she set off to take advantage of her gym membership.

An hour and a half later, she emerged feeling hot and sweaty but with the satisfaction of knowing that the work-out might have gone some way to counteracting the idleness which had become a habit since she had been here.

Turning the corner towards home, she suddenly found herself face to face with Reno.

After just looking at her for a moment, he quietly asked, "What's wrong? Why have you been avoiding me?"

At first she was tempted to just ignore him and escape home but suddenly the anger took over and she blurted out, "How could you? Why did you lie to me? How could you sink so low, just to get in my bed for the night?"

Seeing his stunned look, she was almost ashamed of her outburst until she remembered the woman in the flat with the two young children, blissfully unaware of how her husband was deceiving her.

"What are you talking about?" he asked, a genuine look of puzzlement on his face.

"I found your keys," she spat out. "And took them back to your family, so don't try to pretend to me anymore. I know the truth and never want to see you again. Just leave me alone."

She was taken aback by his roar of laughter and even more surprised when he grabbed her hand and forcibly dragged her along the street until they stood outside the front door to his block of flats.

Ringing the bell outside she had only a minute to wonder why he didn't use his key before someone answered the intercom and saying only, "It's me," heard the door click open and he pulled her up the staircase to his apartment.

As they reached his door, it flew open and two tiny terrors threw themselves at him yelling, "Uncle Reno, Uncle Reno." Scooping them both up he carried them into the flat, passing the woman she had met previously who now beckoned Jane inside.

"They never give the poor man any peace," she smiled. "Although, to be honest, I don't know what we would have done without him."

Leading her into the living room, the first thing Jane noticed was a man with his leg in plaster, stretched out on the settee. "Hello," he called out to her. "You must be Jane. Forgive me for not getting up and thank you so much for returning my keys. As my wife says, I'm forever losing things, but at least this time I had a good excuse."

Seeing her puzzled look, Reno explained, "Paulo had an accident at work and broke his leg. That's why I drove his car home the first time we came here, so that his wife would have it to be able to visit him at the hospital."

At a loss for words and suddenly aware of her dishevelled state, she was relieved when Reno declined the offer to stay for lunch, saying they had some things to sort out.

Wishing Paulo a speedy recovery, she let Reno lead her back downstairs and made no objection when he took her hand to walk back with her to the villa.

"Why didn't you tell me?" she asked when she was slumped into a chair by the pool and after getting them both a cold drink he had sat down next to her.

"Tell you what? That a friend had been involved in an accident? How was I to know you would go to his home, and end up jumping to conclusions?"

Shamefaced, she knew that she was in the wrong, but before she could apologise he grinned at her and said, "Actually, it's nice to know you cared enough to be jealous but next time, ask me about it first before driving me frantic worrying where you have disappeared to."

Looking up at him she asked in a small voice, "Were you really worried about me?"

"What do you think?" he replied softly, before taking her in his arms and kissing her tenderly.

When they finally broke apart she remembered her sweaty state as she had not showered at the gym, intending to freshen up when she got home.

When she mentioned the need for a shower, he said he had a better idea and after a friendly tussle during which he stripped her of her clothes, they both ended up laughing and naked in the pool.

It was some time later that she finally got the opportunity to take her long overdue shower and then she was disappointed to hear him say he would have to go.

Even worse, he would be busy for a few days so wouldn't have the chance to see her.

Although she knew she couldn't monopolise his every waking minute, the house felt empty even when he had only been gone a few minutes.

Putting on some CDs as background music, she spent some time working on her laptop, then used it to call Mr Baker to update him on what she had been doing.

He was delighted to hear from her and pleased with what she had achieved so far. They spent some time discussing the progress from his side and confirmed the details of his forthcoming visit in ten days' time.

When they finished the call she determined to take advantage of Reno being away to work on the project, so that by the time her boss visited, she would be able to present him with a complete outline package.

She couldn't spend all her time working and it occurred to her she could hire a car and maybe spend some time travelling further afield and getting to know the island. Also she needed to confirm arrangements for her party to repay the hospitality she had received. As Mr Baker would be staying overnight, she thought she might combine it with his visit.

Full of enthusiasm again, she started making lists with her usual efficiency before preparing her supper.

When she phoned the couple she had taken the villa from, they said they would be delighted to come but meanwhile insisted she visit them tomorrow for lunch.

After clearing up from her meal, she popped along the road to her neighbours, Gina and Raymond, who also said they would love to come.

She had intended phoning Paula but had no need. She had turned up with Frankie just before Jane left. With their arms wrapped round each other as usual, Paula accepted the invitation on behalf of both of them.

That just left the notary and his wife, who she would phone tomorrow, then contact Gino and Maria.

She did wonder if they would be able to come as they had the restaurant to run and, as it was still quite early, Jane decided to walk along tonight to ask them.

It was a pleasant evening, warm with a slight breeze coming in off the sea. As she strolled along she thought to herself, 'Two lots of exercise in one day, I'm getting good!'

She decided that she would make a point of visiting the gym every couple of days and in-between make sure that she had at least one short, energetic, swim in the pool, rather than just lazing about floating in the water.

In no time at all she found herself outside Gino's and pushing open the door was immediately wrapped in a bear hug by Maria, who scolded her for ignoring them for so long.

She was led to a corner table near the cash register and despite assuring them she had already eaten, had various small plates of finger food placed in front of her to accompany the drink she had ordered.

'So much for my good resolutions,' she thought, unable to resist the delicious nibbles. In between serving the customers, both Gino and Maria sat down at intervals to chat to her and were overjoyed at her invitation.

Covering the restaurant wouldn't be a problem as they regularly left their eldest daughter and her husband in charge when they took a night off.

They were equally delighted when she mentioned that Paula would be there and that she was now seeing Frankie regularly.

"That's wonderful" Maria said. "And it will give Reno some time to concentrate on you," which got Jane wondering if he had seen them, and how much he had told them about their developing relationship.

Eventually she took her leave and began the walk home, her thoughts still on Reno and how long it would be before she saw him again.

Tired after all the unaccustomed exercise, she was soon in bed and fast asleep.

Chapter 25
Preparations

Waking early the next morning to another beautiful day, she had breakfast then walked down to the square to the local tourist information and car hire shop.

Selecting a small Hyundai with a sunroof, she filled in the necessary paperwork for a long-term hire and arranged to pick the car up the following morning.

While she was there she also collected a couple of maps of the island, details of the bus routes and a tourist guide showing places of interest she intended to visit.

Walking up to the main bus depot, she quickly found the right bus to take her to the village where Mr and Mrs Melina, the previous owners of the villa were now living. Although the ancient bus looked as if it would never make it, she enjoyed the drive through vineyards and fields until the bus dropped her, about twenty minutes later, in the centre of a modern, bustling, town.

Consulting the directions she had been given, she took the main road leading out of town and soon found herself in a prestigious tree-lined avenue with a street sign confirming it was the road she was looking for.

She noticed that most of the villas had names rather than numbers but she had no need to worry about finding the correct house as she heard her name being called. Looking up she saw Mrs Melina herself walking towards her accompanied by a woman she assumed was her daughter.

After making the introductions, they walked a few yards back up the road and stopped at a large house set in extensive grounds with a smaller self-contained building set off to one side.

As they went through the main gate Mr Melina appeared from the smaller house and welcomed her to their new home.

Although it was a lot smaller than the villa, the couple had already added their own personal touches so it was a charming retirement home. It was easy for them to manage and they had their daughter next door should they need help in an emergency but still had the privacy to live their own lives.

After they had showed her around, their daughter returned to say that lunch was nearly ready. She was given a guided tour of the main house and then led into the garden where a long table was set out under the trees, filled to overflowing with a variety of cold food.

As they sat down and she was poured a large glass of chilled white wine, she was joined by various grandchildren and their friends, as well as their son-in-law and a few of his work colleagues.

The lunch took on a party atmosphere and she was made to feel totally at home in the large family group. Some of the teenagers shyly tried out their English on her and wanted to know all about London, which they wanted to visit once they had broken up from school and colleges for the long summer holidays.

The hours flew past and before she knew it 6 o'clock had been and gone. Reluctantly she said she must take her leave.

Despite their protests, she insisted she must go and some of the teenagers immediately offered to walk back with her to catch the bus.

Although it was now getting dark, she enjoyed the drive home through the darkened fields and villages. She surprised herself by the intense feeling of homecoming she experienced as the villa came into view following a short walk back from the bus stop. Letting herself in, she took a moment to gaze round the villa and think how lucky she was to have found such a perfect home.

She took pleasure in cutting up some onions, garlic and ginger which she mixed with some beautiful large red tomatoes and fresh herbs, to make a sauce to go with the chicken breasts she would have for supper later.

Even making a dressing of olive oil and lemon juice to go with the salad, she realised how much she was enjoying preparing fresh food instead of just relying on jars and packets from the local London supermarket.

Although she enjoyed the excitement of busy London life, with its theatres, restaurants and entertainment all within easy reach, she had already started to adapt to the slower pace of life. She found that the local shops could still provide everything she needed without the stress of the metropolis.

More and more she was beginning to realise that she could easily make this her home for life, especially with the right man by her side.

She settled down for a peaceful evening, turning on the television and finding an English channel to catch up on the news, then spent some time reading her book while she ate her late supper with some CDs playing in the background.

Feeling relaxed and totally contented with her new life, she took herself off to bed, and slept like a log.

Chapter 26
Exploring

Waking with the sun the next morning, Jane kept to her resolve and did a few lengths of the pool before making her breakfast.

Then, after showering and dressing for the day as a tourist, she walked down to the square to collect her hire car.

She found it easy to drive after the much larger one she had been used to in England and felt quite adventurous as she headed out of town to pastures new, stopping now and then to consult her map or just gaze at the scenery.

There weren't many signposts and she soon found the easiest way to navigate was to head in the general direction of a town or village, then follow her nose until she saw a major church which was likely to be in the centre of the town square.

Although not a fanatic churchgoer, she found the churches beautiful, both the large, ornate, town ones, but even more so the ones in the smaller fishing villages which had a personality of their own, fitting the local environment.

Following a steep winding road down to one small village by the sea, she was amazed at the amount of traffic on the road. Going with the flow and finding a parking space in the village square, she got out and followed the crowd down to the harbour. She realised that she was at the tail end of a religious procession. A large statue of the local saint was being carried on the shoulders of local fishermen to be blessed at a ceremony amongst the boats, before hundreds of flower petals were thrown into the water to give thanks for the prosperity of the fishing season.

After the gravity of the service, the village erupted into a joyful celebration with the local bars overflowing, colourful parades with decorated floats and people wearing both bizarre and traditional costumes.

The air was resonant with the sounds of competing brass bands from the local clubs, each trying to outdo the other with both the skill of their music and the amount of noise they could make.

Everywhere she could smell the enticing aromas of food being cooked on the various stalls set up along the roadside, as well as other stalls doing a roaring trade selling traditional sweets and cakes.

As day turned to evening, the sky was lit up with an explosion of fireworks and she jostled happily with the friendly crowd, joining in their oohs and aahs as each display tried to outdo the previous one.

Eventually she made her way back to where she had parked her car, and tired but contented, managed to find her route home.

Chapter 27
Plans and practicalities

Keeping to her new resolution, Jane had only an orange juice before making her way to the gym for an hour's exercise. Then, after a revitalising shower, sat down to enjoy the fresh rolls she had picked up at the bakers on the way back, washed down with a large mug of coffee.

Her mind now fully alert, she settled down to do a few hours' work on her computer. Feeling justified that both her brain and her body had done enough for the day, she had a light lunch then drove the short distance to the large resort further along the coast. After all the driving she had done yesterday, it was nice to know that there was a sandy beach so conveniently close as a change from the pool.

Being in a much more touristy area there were fewer local families and she amused herself trying to identify all the different accents.

She easily recognised Italian, Spanish, French and German and something she was pretty sure was Russian but others she had to give up on, although she guessed they could be from some of the eastern European nations.

There seemed to be a lot of students who, when not in their own groups, used English as a common language, especially to the shopkeepers on the main road and in the cafés and kiosks lining the beach.

Buying a local paper later in the afternoon, she was not surprised to see various advertisements for language schools, particularly in that area.

Her interest was caught by an article in the 'What's On' section, describing an open air theatre production taking place that evening at a venue which she was fairly sure was close to Gino's restaurant.

She had noticed the large building with its flags and bunting on her previous walks but never stopped to look closely.

Turning her attention back to the serious business of doing nothing, she stretched out on her sun lounger and spent the afternoon topping up her tan, in between dips in the sea when it got too hot.

As she was leaving she saw a billboard outside one of the shops advertising the theatre and going in to enquire, she confirmed it was where she had thought and ended up buying a ticket for guaranteed seating.

The shopkeeper was eager to tell her more about it, especially as her daughter-in-law was one of the performers. Jane discovered the company put on regular performances during the summer months.

The venue was an old Roman amphitheatre, with the stone steps higher up forming the cheaper seats and proper chairs set out lower down, nearer the beach where the main stage was set up.

In the winter the troupe moved to the proper indoor theatre, which, following the shopkeeper's pointing finger, Jane could just make out in the distance, partly hidden behind the large stores in the main shopping precinct.

Smiling and wishing her a pleasant evening, the shopkeeper told Jane that personally, she much preferred the open-air venue and was sure she would enjoy herself.

Arriving home, Jane laid out some white cotton trousers to wear later that evening, together with a short-sleeved gypsy style top in a mixture of greens and blues which complemented the colours in the earrings Reno had bought her.

Realising she would be close to the evening sea breezes, she added a loose, flowing, dark blue cardigan, in a silky cotton fabric, especially as it might be quite late by the time the performance ended.

After taking a leisurely bath, she applied copious amounts of body cream to rehydrate her skin, which was still warm and glowing after her day in the sun.

Realising that time was slipping away, she decided to have an early supper at Gino's rather than waste time cooking. Dressing quickly she checked that she had her ticket and set off to walk along the coast road.

Passing the theatre building, she saw that the performance was due to start at 8 o'clock and as Gino's was only about 100 yards further along the road the timing would work out perfectly.

As it was still quite early, the restaurant wasn't busy when she arrived and she was soon enjoying a light evening meal, washed down with the ubiquitous half bottle of wine.

Using the ladies' toilet to freshen up, Jane left around 7.45, bade goodbye to Gino and Maria and made her way along the road to the theatre, which was already crowded with people going to watch the performance.

She was shown to her seat in a good position, close to the front of the action and off to one side, in the midst of mainly local people, everything from grandmas in family groups, to teenagers laughing and joking with their friends.

The atmosphere was electric and noisy but the sound died down and a hush descended as the curtain on the makeshift stage rose promptly at 8 o'clock.

The actors spoke in the local language but with a prompt half hidden behind the curtain giving an English translation, she soon became engrossed in the performance.

About 9.30 there was an interval, when she joined the many other patrons to queue for a drink at the outlets dotted around the area selling refreshments. She bought herself a hot chocolate and couldn't resist a packet of some local delicacies to nibble on.

As she was making her way back, she thought she spied Reno at the far side, accompanied by a woman several inches shorter than him, with a dark complexion and brown curly hair.

At first she was tempted to go over to where they were heading but at that moment the loudspeaker asked people to resume their seats for the second act. Berating herself for being a jealous fool, she went back to her seat.

She soon became engrossed in the second half and when the production finished around 10.45 she joined enthusiastically in the applause from the audience.

Making her way out through the throng, she did look around to see if she could them again but the crowd was so dense, even if he had been there, she was unlikely to be able to pick him out again.

Despite that, she had thoroughly enjoyed the evening, and arriving home shortly after 11, she didn't even bother to make herself a nightcap but collecting a glass of water, went straight to bed.

Chapter 28
Reunions and revelations

Jane woke the next morning with the haunting theme song from the night before echoing through her consciousness and the sun once again beaming through the unshuttered blinds.

She found herself humming the melody as she made her breakfast and went to eat it by the pool.

When her mobile rang, she wondered who could be phoning her so early and for a moment was worried that it was Mr Baker who had encountered some problem with her work.

Answering somewhat apprehensively, she immediately recognised the deep, sexy, voice as Reno's and hoped he wasn't aware of how her heart was fluttering just hearing him say "Good morning."

Her heart beat even faster when to her enquiry, "Where are you?" he replied, "Outside the front door. Are you going to let me in?"

As it was closer, instead of going through the house, she took the path leading round the side of the villa to come up behind him.

He must have heard her footsteps as he turned suddenly and with a big smile on his face, went to pull her into his arms.

Laughing, she ducked away, calling, "Not today, thank you," and took off running back the way she had come, with him in hot pursuit.

Her recent training must have been more effective than she thought, or maybe he had just been taken by surprise, for she made it all the way back to the grassy area near the pool before he caught up with her.

Teasing and trying to dive under his arm, she lost her footing, and grabbing hold of him for support, dragged him down with her, until they were both rolling around on the soft grass.

"Right Miss. You need to be punished," he said, as they lay there and gently drawing her head towards him, kissed her soundly.

"If that's what I get when I don't see you for a few days, you should go away more often," she said softly, once she had regained her breath.

Laughing, he helped her to her feet, then brushing themselves off, they regained some dignity by sitting at the table by the pool while she finished her breakfast.

"So what have you been doing with yourself?" he asked and she found herself telling him about hiring a car and the various trips she had made, including the theatre trip last night.

"Yes, it was good wasn't it, we enjoyed it," he said at one point and she immediately thought 'Who is 'we'?'

Instead of letting her jealousy show, which had caused misunderstandings before, she merely said, "I thought I saw you, but it was so crowded I couldn't be certain."

When he asked her if she had found time to do any work on her project in the middle of her hectic social life, she told him it was going well, and that her boss would be coming over the following week.

That reminded her of the house warming party she was throwing and she tentatively asked if he would be free to come.

He said he would do his very best to be there but he had a lot on this week, especially as he had to make some airport trips. Some people were arriving from Canada and he might be tied up chauffeuring them around for a few days.

Again she felt the twinge of jealousy and realised that, as usual, he gave very little away about his private life.

Realising the flat she thought was his actually belonged to Paulo and his family, it occurred to her that she didn't even know where he lived.

Before she could ask him, he had pulled her up and saying "Come on, lazybones, time for a swim," had stripped off to the trunks he was wearing under his clothes. He had already done a couple of strong lengths of the pool before she quickly changed and joined him.

After some serious swimming, they fooled and splashed around for a while before he got out and drying himself off, glanced at his watch and said he would have to be leaving soon.

Her disappointment must have shown, because after a moment's hesitation, he asked if she was free on Sunday for a family lunch.

Smiling when she accepted immediately, he warned her that she might regret it later, once she had been regaled for hours with the stories of elderly aunts, or been made to play interminable games by hordes of young nieces and nephews.

Hearing she was looking forward to it, he warned her to wear something that was not easily ruined and arranged to pick her up about midday.

Then, with a quick kiss, he was gone.

Suppressing her disappointment at not having Reno's company for the day, Jane made herself some lunch then spent the afternoon working.

At least she had Sunday to look forward to, when she would see him again and hopefully find out more about him when she saw him in his family environment.

Taking a break in the late afternoon, she popped down to the square to buy a few groceries she had run short of.

Before heading home she sat on a bench by the sea for a while, just watching the world go by and the sun go down.

Hearing her name called, she looked up to see one of her other neighbours, who she had met at Gina and Raymond's party, with various members of her family, most of whom were carrying cool boxes or carrier bags of food.

Hearing she had nothing special to do, they insisted she join them for their barbecue on the beach, as they couldn't possibly leave her to eat on her own.

With all her protests overruled, she popped back to the shop to buy a couple of bottles of wine as her contribution. She returned to find the family spread out in front of the open door of a building set into the stone, one of a row of huts set along the beach. She had noticed them before from the road above but had assumed they were some sort of storage blocks, or perhaps garages for keeping the boats in during the winter months.

Peering inside, she saw they were in fact small, but well equipped, beach huts, complete with air conditioning, lights and even a sink with running water.

She was soon involved in carrying out the various folding tables and chairs which had been stored inside and setting them out on the stone area in front of the hut. Meanwhile the men had set up the barbecue and the women were placing the bread and salads on the larger tables.

The younger ones were more interested in getting the music going, or playing with the large beach ball, but were called back at intervals to help fetch and carry.

Despite all the noise and chaos, in a surprisingly short time everything was organised and the enticing smell of burgers, sausages and onions wafting from the barbecue, was making her feel hungry.

After handing out the paper napkins and plastic plates to the elderly lady who everyone addressed as 'Nana', she was told to help herself from the table and grab a chair otherwise she would end up standing and starving.

Taking them at her word she found herself a chair on the edge of the sand and was soon in conversation with some of the other ladies, many of whom she had not met before.

By now she was becoming used to perfect strangers asking the usual questions: 'How many children did she have? Was she married? Where was her young man?'

Even so, she was quite relieved when the men caused a diversion by bringing over trays of hot food from the barbecue and the teenagers were instructed to make sure everyone had a drink.

She learnt that this was a common event at weekends during the summer months, when the women delegated the cooking to the men and were able to sit and enjoy the fresh sea breezes, rather than being cooped up in the kitchen.

It was very much open house, with people coming and going at various times during the evening, some stopping to eat, others just joining them for a drink or a chat.

She enjoyed the informal family style atmosphere and was just starting to wonder if Reno's party the following day would be on similar lines, when some of the younger ones insisted she join them, to even up the numbers for their boisterous game of beach volleyball.

Kicking off her shoes she was pleased that, despite being the eldest, she didn't let the side down and even joined her team-mates in laughingly teasing the boys when the girls were victorious.

Flopping back in her seat exhausted, she welcomed the long, cool glass of wine that was handed to her and the chance to take a break while she got her breath back.

She was flattered when a while later, the teenagers asked if she wanted to join them, as they were off to meet some friends at an open air disco further along the beach. Thanking them sincerely, but saying maybe another time, she felt overwhelmed at the way she had been so readily accepted into the community where she now felt totally at home.

Looking back, it seemed unbelievable how much her life had changed in less than two months.

She had a new look, a new job, a new home, a new life, new friends and even, she hoped, a new man. Everything she could possibly wish for.

When the family started packing up, sometime after 10 p.m., she helped store away the furniture in the hut, then walked back with the others to their respective homes. Calling goodnight and thanking them for their hospitality, she walked the few yards further to her own villa, where the quiet of the house seemed strange after all the noise of the evening.

Stripping off her somewhat sandy clothes, she took a quick shower, changed into a loose towelling wrap and putting on some soft background music, took her coffee to sit at her usual spot on the patio.

Before long she found herself yawning and took herself off to bed. After all the fresh air and exercise of the day, no sooner had her head touched the pillow than she was sound asleep.

Chapter 29
Meeting the family

Waking early the next morning, she did a few laps of the pool before having her breakfast, then turned on her laptop to catch up with some e-mails.

She sent a few quick replies to various friends, then a longer one updating her sister on what she had been doing and asking how the new house and Mark's new job was going.

At first the weather had been a bit overcast and, although still warm, she detected some rain in the air.

She hoped it wouldn't spoil the lunch party, but nothing would mar her pleasure at seeing Reno again, although she was a little apprehensive about what his family would be like and if they would take to her.

Suddenly she felt the first few spots of warm, soft, rain, which quickly became heavier until it was raining in earnest.

'Typical,' she thought to herself. 'The first rain in weeks, and it has to be today.'

She needn't have worried. After about five minutes, the rain stopped, the sun came out and the only sign of the recent shower was the sweet, fresh, smell of the flowers and grass after their refreshing drink.

She had considered wearing trousers but now that the sun looked as if it had settled in for the day, changed her mind and picked out a sleeveless cotton dress with a wide belt and a colourful abstract pattern over a plain navy background.

Adding navy sandals, stud earrings and a touch of make-up, she transferred her keys and other essentials to a navy shoulder bag and she was ready.

Noticing that she had around twenty minutes to wait, she wandered about aimlessly for a while until, in an effort to quell the butterflies in her stomach, she took out her 'To do' list and started planning for her party the following weekend.

Her mind distracted, she was startled by the bell ringing about fifteen minutes later and she opened the door to see Reno, looking as good as he had in her dreams and every inch as sexy.

"You look perfect," he said, as he gave her a tender kiss and putting down her notebook, she picked up her handbag and they walked hand in hand out of the house,

Although they didn't say much on the ten-minute walk that followed it was a comfortable silence. Both of them were deep in thought but the contented smile on his face meant that words weren't necessary.

All too soon he opened what appeared to be the back gate of an ancient estate and she found herself in the gardens of an exclusive and beautifully converted hotel.

Immediately they came into view he was assaulted by a host of young children, all talking at once and vying to be the one to hold his hand.

Smiling, she had to relinquish 'Uncle Reno' to her younger competitors and followed him over the lawn to where tables were set out with beautiful bone china and crystal glasses for lunch.

Managing to shake off his nieces and nephews, she was glad when he took her hand to start the introductions to the adults. She found she was trembling at the prospect of finally finding out more about this enigmatic man.

There was no mistaking the charming, grey-haired, older version of Reno who he introduced as his father, or his good looking but not so dynamic younger brother.

She sensed an air of sophistication and old family affluence in the paternal side of his family, so she was somewhat surprised when she was introduced to his mother.

Although she was beautifully and expensively dressed, she had the aura and rosy-cheeked face of a country lass.

In contrast to her husband, she was short and stocky, but Jane could see that although she was now middle-aged, in her youth she must have been a stunning natural beauty. With those genes, it was no wonder that Reno had turned out so well, combining the best assets from both his parents to make a perfect offspring.

It was also obvious that despite her diminutive stature and without distracting from his father's masculine role, his mother was the head of the family household and her husband still adored her.

Next she was introduced to his sister, who had just arrived from Canada to join the family celebrations. This gave her a clue as to his recent unavailability and hints at airport excursions, quelling her earlier secret jealousy.

After being introduced to various other family members, she found herself seated beside Reno's father and was embarrassed that she had come empty-handed when she found out the reason for the lunch was to celebrate his birthday.

Trying to apologise, she was put at her ease by the older man telling her the company of a beautiful lady was the perfect present and at least his eldest son had inherited his own good taste in women.

Laughing as he gallantly kissed her hand, she looked up to see Reno smiling down at them and saying he was going to drag her away before the old man stole her from him.

At that moment a gong sounded and an immaculately dressed headwaiter invited them to take their seats as lunch was served.

Settling her in a seat a short way down the table, Reno went back to escort his mother to her place at the head of the table next to his father.

Before he returned she was joined by another female younger version of Reno, who introduced herself as his sister Katerine, but known to the family as Kate.

Although more subtle in her questioning than some of the older ladies had been, Jane still found herself answering questions as to whether she had been married, children, and how long she had known Reno?

Apologising for being so direct, Kate told her that it was normal practice for a new girlfriend to be interrogated by families, and if Jane thought she was intrusive, wait until some of the older aunts got her cornered!

Her sister-in-law Rita, sitting opposite, who had been listening to the conversation, joined in and laughingly agreed she still had nightmares recalling the third degree she had undergone when she started dating Reno's brother.

It was bad enough with ordinary families but obviously this family's circumstances made it ten times harder.

Puzzled, Jane was just going to ask her what she meant about this family being special, when Reno returned and smilingly told them to give the poor girl a break before she tried to make a run for it.

The moment was broken by the staff beginning to serve their first course and the conversation turned to more general themes.

The food was delicious and beautifully presented and she noticed that every now and then the maître d' would confer with Reno to ensure everything was satisfactory and there were no matters that needed addressing, or to check on timings.

Although the conversation and laughter flowed easily, she was aware of him subtly changing the subject whenever she asked what someone did for a living, or discussions about the family became more detailed.

All she found out was that his father was nearing retirement and the family were very close knit and often worked together.

It was only when he was called away for a few minutes and she remarked aloud on the beautiful hotel and whether it was privately owned or part of a chain, that Rita offered some information. It was part of the family owned group, which included the hotel where she had been staying, plus several others Jane had noticed while exploring the island.

It seemed they specialised in buying up old buildings of character, such as manor or farm houses, or the occasional castle, and sympathetically converting them to modern 5 star hotels, whilst ensuring they retained their individuality and original charm.

It was only when Rita started saying that most of the family were involved in one way or another, that Jane thought she saw Kate give her a warning glance.

Almost as if she was changing the subject, Rita volunteered that the men, whilst still in their teens, traditionally learned various skills and crafts from their fathers and older family members.

Kate told her that her own husband was a talented stonemason and although he rarely took on larger projects now, he still produced beautifully carved and ornate ornaments or designs in the traditional style.

"What about Reno?" Jane asked, "Does he have a particular speciality?"

"Reno is jack of all trades," she heard him say from behind her, where he had returned unnoticed. "But for now he is chief toastmaster."

"Ladies and Gentleman," he called out. "Could I have your attention for a moment? First of all I'd like to thank you all for coming today, especially those who have travelled from the other side of the world and I hope you have enjoyed yourselves. We all know how much it means to the old man to have you all here to help celebrate his birthday."

"Not so much of the old," called a voice from the head of the table. "You might think you're all grown up, but I can still give you a spanking if you get too lippy!"

"Sorry Pa," said Reno, amongst the laughter. "Friends and family, will you please raise your glasses to wish 'the young man' a very happy birthday. I won't tell you how old he is in case I get a whipping, just that it's got a nought on the end and his bus pass is ready."

To a chorus of happy birthdays and the clink of raised glasses, Reno resumed his seat as a cake in the shape of a castle, complete with turrets and battlements, was ceremoniously carried to the top of the table.

There was more laughter as Reno's father made a mess of cutting the cake. Teasing about useless men who could build a hotel but were hopeless in the kitchen, his wife took over before it became, as she put it, an ancient crumbling ruin.

A line of children and adults made their way to the top table to present their gifts and good wishes.

They were led by a little girl of no more than three, who presented Reno's mother with a huge bouquet, because, "You deserve it for having to look after Grandpa."

Grandpa immediately grabbed her, put her over his knee and tickled until she was giggling and had given him a big kiss as a forfeit.

Then Nana said she deserved a big kiss too, which she got after the toddler had climbed up and settled herself in her lap.

"If I give you some flowers, will I get a big kiss too?" Reno whispered in Jane's ear.

"Only if you're a good boy, and eat your greens," she smiled back.

A few minutes later Reno got up and she laughed out loud when he returned chewing on a cabbage leaf and presented her with a few bedraggled daisies.

Keeping her promise, she too had to pay her forfeit.

At about 7 o'clock the party started to break up, especially as some of the younger ones had missed their afternoon nap and were worn out with all the excitement.

As Reno was busy packing up the presents and sorting out transport for the various guests, she assured him she could see herself home and after saying her goodbyes, made her way home alone.

After the heavy lunch she wasn't that hungry, so just made herself a small snack before opening up her computer to catch up on work and correspondence.

There was a very positive update from Mr Baker, full of plans as to the way the business was developing and a rather disturbing e-mail from Jena, which without giving too much away sounded rather downbeat.

Thinking of her sister got Jane comparing the happy family atmosphere of the afternoon and turned her thinking to the information and reticence that the conversation had divulged.

It had become obvious that the family were all involved in the hotel trade and she assumed that, with their various skills, the men were responsible for the building and possibly even the design of the projects, so why the hesitation in talking about it? Surely they weren't ashamed of being working men when the end results were of such a high calibre.

Maybe they thought that with her designer clothes, staying at expensive hotels and no obvious source of income, that she had private means to enable her to buy the villa and spend her days without obviously working from nine to five.

Deciding straight answers from both her sister and Reno were preferable to analysing things to death and jumping to the wrong conclusions, she prepared for an early night.

She was just locking the front door when the sound of the bell made her jump.

"Who is it?" she called.

"It's only me," came the reply. "Did I disturb you?"

As she let him in, she thought, 'You always disturb me, but not in the way that you mean.'

It was only as he followed her into the light of the lounge, and she saw his admiring glance sweep over her from head to toe that she realised she was wearing only a very short, sheer, night-gown.

"Very nice," he said softly, then proceeded to kiss her until her mind went blank and her ears were ringing.

"Were you in bed?" he asked when he finally released her.

When she told him she was just going, he offered to tuck her in and taking her by the hand led her up to her bedroom.

An hour later there was no question of the bedclothes being tucked in, as after quickly stripping off his clothes he had joined her in bed and made love to her until she was breathless.

At first she had been surprised at his passion, but soon found her ardour matching his until they both collapsed, exhausted.

Feeling totally sated and cosseted, wrapped in his arms, her only reply to his whispered, "Can I stay?" was to snuggle up closer to him, and soon she was fast asleep with his broad chest as her pillow.

Chapter 30
Dreams and realities

Opening her eyes and stretching languidly the next morning, Jane felt as if something was missing.

Her mind went back to last night and for a moment she felt as if she had dreamt the whole thing, until she smelt the tantalising aromas of bacon and coffee wafting from the kitchen.

Splashing her face with water, she threw on a cotton shift and went downstairs to find Reno looking totally at home, frying pan in hand and a tea towel tied round his waist.

"Morning, sleepy-head," he smiled as he saw her. "Ready for some breakfast?"

"Um, please," she replied, thinking not many men could look so sexy first thing in the morning, wearing a tea towel.

As if he could read her thoughts, he gave her a quick kiss and carried the plates to the patio, where he had already set out the cutlery, fresh orange juice, coffee and warm rolls.

"I could get used to being spoilt like this," she said, almost to herself.

"Just say the word and I'm your slave to command," he replied seriously, then broke the moment by whipping off the tea-towel, pretending to dust off the chair and seating her like an over fussy waiter.

Keeping the mood light, she pretended to look down her nose as she muttered about hired help taking liberties by eating at the same table as the Lady of the Manor. Fleetingly she caught his strange look before he started fawning over her again, joking that, as the official food taster, he had to make sure everything was perfect before sullying Modom's lips.

True to his mood he grabbed the piece of bread from her hand and started nibbling it, teasing her by waving it under her nose before moving it out of reach.

Trying to grab it back, in the mock fight that ensued she ended up sitting on his lap, with him feeding her as if he really was her devoted slave.

Teasing that the food wasn't bad for a beginner, she commented how perfect the cuisine had been yesterday and asked if his parents had enjoyed it.

Smiling, he told her that they would be happy with bread and cheese providing they had the family round them and that she had earned him some brownie points as they had all thought she was perfect.

Talking about the various relatives she had met, she casually mentioned that they all seemed to work closely together and seemed to know a lot about the various hotels. At first she thought he wasn't going to comment, then he explained that his great grandfather had started working for a small hotel many years ago and from humble beginnings, the group had expanded until they were now multinational.

Over the years, most of the family had joined the business in some form or another, from the early days when his grandmother had done the cleaning and his grandfather the maintenance, to now, when the younger ones had helped develop the computer systems.

He had spent several years travelling for the company, looking for suitable sites abroad to add to the chain, but for now his globetrotting days were over and he was settled permanently on the island.

She reminded him of the first time she had seen him, emerging from under the floorboards, covered with dust, totally unlike the smart suited business executive flying first class.

Laughing, he told her the hotel she had first stayed in belonged to the corporation and that if something needed doing, it was his job to do it.

He asked her how things were progressing with her old boss and seemed genuinely interested in his plans and her involvement, joking she had better be careful or she too would be seconded into doing the marketing for the hotels.

Then saying he had to work this afternoon, but for now he had the morning off and was going to make the most of it, he stripped off and jumped into the pool as naked as the day he was born.

For a few minutes she watched him powering up and down then with a sense of freedom, she threw off her own clothes and joined him in the water.

All too soon he had to leave and reluctantly they dried off and got dressed, then after helping her clear the breakfast things, with a glance at his watch and a quick kiss he was gone and she was alone.

At first she wandered about just missing Reno's presence, then pulling herself together made her plans for the rest of the day.

Talking about her work she remembered guiltily that she had not so far kept her promise to Joseph to help him computerise his collection of books.

Leaving the house she stopped at the bakers to buy a couple of pasties for her lunch, then made her way to the bookshop.

Looking through the open door, at first she thought the room was empty but as her eyes adjusted to the dim interior after the glare of the sun outside, she saw him sitting towards the back sorting through a pile of cardboard boxes.

Noticing her, he stood up and came towards her and greeted her warmly.

She apologised for not coming sooner and was amazed that he obviously remembered her after only one meeting and was delighted at her renewed offer of assistance.

While she helped him unpack the boxes, they chatted about what sort of system he needed to catalogue his stock and the best way to set it up.

Leading her to his desk, he showed her the very modern computer, scanner, printer and photocopier, which all looked in pristine condition.

She noticed with amusement none of them were turned on and the desk was covered with various notebooks with sheets of handwritten lists.

Turning the computer on, she noticed some files which were a half-hearted attempt to start categorising but which looked as if they had been abandoned in frustration.

Accepting her suggestion that they start from scratch using a more appropriate package, instead of just making lists, he watched, intrigued, as she converted the information in his existing files and saved them in a folder for later use.

As she started setting up the new database and allocating various headings, he quickly picked up the basis of what she was doing and asked if it was possible to add other categories which would help him identify and trace his stock more quickly.

His pleasure obvious as the suggestions were incorporated and the structure quickly took shape, he told her he was a fool to have struggled for so long and should have done this years ago.

Looking round the crowded room, Jane doubted whether he appreciated just how long it would take to input the vast, ever changing, stock and wondered just what she had got herself into.

Deciding the less changeable library section would be the best place to start, she copied the outline and explained how the two saved folders corresponded to his fiction and non-fiction bookshelves.

Taking a break from the computer, they examined the room itself and came up with a plan for re-organising the shelves and bookcases into a more logical sequence. Assuring her he had an army of helpers amongst his relatives and school pupils to carry out the manual work, he was overwhelming in his gratitude for her help in getting him started.

Feeling decidedly grubby, she found herself promising to call back in a day or two to start the task of actually cataloguing his collection.

Returning home she told herself she had earned a break and changing quickly into her bikini, spent an hour swimming in the pool, before collapsing, exhausted, onto the lounger to catch the last rays of the dying sun.

Gradually becoming aware of feeling slightly chilly, she opened her eyes to realise she must have fallen asleep as it was now early evening.

Going indoors, a warm bath soon revived her and she gave some thought to her evening meal.

Feeling too lazy to bother to cook, she decided to eat out, although it crossed her mind that if Reno did come back that evening he would find no one at home.

Thinking back, she became conscious that he never actually made arrangements as to when he would next see her; always just turning up at different times during the day or night.

Decision made, she got dressed and started walking towards the square.

Feeling like a change, she didn't stop at either of the two Mediterranean restaurants she had visited before, but taking some side roads, ended up in another small square she hadn't been to before.

Apart from a few shops that were closed and shuttered for the night, she passed two small bars and what appeared to be a social club which, from the noise coming through the open doors, was doing a roaring business.

Noticing more lights a little further on, she found herself looking up at the awnings of a Chinese, an Indian and a Thai restaurant, in close proximity, with an Italian pizzeria and a Spanish tapas bar a little further along.

Not feeling in the mood for boisterous company, she chose the quieter Thai, and entering the dim interior was shown to a secluded table towards the rear.

After making her selection from the menu, she spent a few minutes looking round at her surroundings. The ornate carvings, decoration and traditional pictures gave the place an ambience which reminded her of the antique shop in London where she had spent many happy hours browsing.

It seemed impossible that it was only a few months ago; it felt like another lifetime.

Although the restaurant gradually got busier, the clientele was mainly couples, talking quietly to each other, the younger ones holding hands across the table, rather than the large family parties she had become used to lately.

She enjoyed the meal and the unrushed, tranquil, atmosphere gave her a chance to sit and think.

Naturally her mind drifted back towards Reno, who despite all she had learnt about him today, still remained something of an enigma.

She also thought of the older two men, Mr Baker and Joseph, and how in their own ways they were so alike in their passion for their respective businesses.

She thought they would get on well and decided she would take the opportunity to introduce them to each other when Mr Baker came over in a few days' time.

That reminded her, she still had a few things to sort out for the party and she determined to spend tomorrow finalising the arrangements.

Her mind full of plans, she paid her bill and began walking home.

Deep in thought, she became aware of a limousine passing her on the narrow street and although the windows were blacked out, for some reason she thought one of the occupants sitting next to the partially open window was Reno.

Although she turned her head to check, the car was already some way up the road and by the time she reached the villa, she had decided it was just wishful thinking.

He was still on her mind when she got into bed, but gradually her thoughts relaxed and she drifted into sleep.

Chapter 31
Plans and organisation

Jane woke the next morning from a confused dream where she was working for Reno, tidying his shelves, while Mr Baker and Joseph were cooking a meal in the swimming pool.

Shaking her head at herself, she had a quick breakfast before making her way to the gym for a quick workout to shake the cobwebs out of her brain.

On the way back she stopped at the butcher's and placed her order for the joint of beef she intended to cook on Saturday, then at the grocer's for the potatoes and vegetables and finally at the fishmonger's to order some unbelievably large prawns to use for a starter.

A final call at the baker's to buy some fresh rolls for lunch and place her order, which he promised to deliver around lunchtime on Saturday and she felt satisfied with her morning's work.

Returning home she spent some time on her laptop, putting the final touches to her project which she would be discussing when Mr Baker arrived, then, after a light supper, read for a while before going off to bed, still with no sign or sight of Reno.

Chapter 32
More organisation

Waking early the next morning, Jane had a quick swim in the pool, then spent an hour or so catching up with e-mails from Jena and confirming final arrangements with Mr Baker about the arrival time of his flight and collecting him from the airport.

Then, after an early lunch, she walked down to the bookstore to keep her promise to Joseph.

She was amazed at the transformation and the amount that had already been achieved in clearing space and reorganising the bookshelves.

Obviously he hadn't under estimated the willingness of his army of helpers, as the rear of the shop now contained his reference and non-fiction books, arranged in order of subject, with the shelves neatly labelled.

Opening up the files she had saved, Jane was soon engrossed in working her way through the different sections, allocating a reference number and cataloguing the books by subject, author and title.

She was surprised how quickly the time had flown when Joseph told her that was enough for today as it was already nearly six.

With his thanks ringing in her ears, she promised to come back to do some more next week and walked back to the villa.

After preparing a lasagne and salad for her evening meal, Jane poured herself a glass of wine and did a final check of her list for the weekend.

Happy that everything was under control, she ate on the patio, washed up and settled down to watch a film on the television for a few hours, before preparing for bed.

Still no word from Reno.

Chapter 33
Preparations

Waking early the next morning, Jane had a quick breakfast then went through the whole house, cleaning, dusting and hoovering until every surface was gleaming and welcoming.

Deciding she had no time for the gym, she spent an hour in the pool on some strenuous laps before showering and having a light lunch.

Although the trip to the airport would take less than half an hour, she didn't want to keep her boss waiting, and by 2 o'clock she was already on her way to meet his flight which was due in at three.

With little traffic on the road, easy parking and still some forty minutes to wait, she went into the café. Ordering a coffee she sat down at a table by the large glass window, where she could see the planes arriving.

When her mobile rang, her first thought was that the plane had arrived early but glancing at the information board, she saw that it was due shortly although it had not yet landed.

Answering her phone, she immediately recognised the deep voice asking how she was and apologising for not having contacted her sooner but he had been tied up on business for the last few days.

Replying she was fine, she was on the point of saying to Reno that she was at the airport, when he told her that he only had a minute but just wanted to let her know that he would definitely see her the following evening for her party.

She could hear someone calling him in the background and before she could ask him anything more, he said, "Sorry, I've got to go, see you tomorrow," and with that she was listening to a dialling tone.

Not sure whether to be pleased he had made contact, or annoyed at the brevity of the conversation, she put her mobile back in her bag, finished her coffee and walked over to the arrivals area.

She had only a few minutes to wait before her old boss emerged, looking sun tanned and fit and surprised her by greeting her with a warm kiss on both cheeks, more like a friend than an ex-employee.

His only luggage being his laptop and an overnight flight bag, they were soon back in the car and leaving the airport.

On the way they talked about the new business and he surprised her by admitting how relieved he had been when she had agreed to help him, as up to that point he hadn't been certain about going ahead with it.

Now, with her contribution, things had moved on at an incredible pace and everything was set for the launch the following week.

They were still chatting when they arrived back at the villa and he told her how pleased he was to hear that she was happy and settled in her new life, as he still had some feelings of guilt about the way his sons had treated her.

She couldn't help a feeling of pride as she showed him round and he complimented her on her beautiful home.

When he asked if she had actually bought it or was renting, it reminded her that she needed to see the notary to finalise the purchase, as subconsciously she had already made her decision that this was to be her permanent home.

He refused her offer of something to eat as he had had lunch on the plane but said he would love a proper cup of tea, something he had missed since being in Spain.

Luckily her local shop stocked his favourite brand of tea and she had got in some supplies.

While he was freshening up in the spare bedroom she had prepared for him, she made the brew and set it out on the patio, together with a plate of his favourite biscuits.

They spent the rest of the afternoon going over the business details and by 7 o'clock were both confident that they had covered all aspects and now it was in the hands of fate.

He insisted on treating her to a celebratory meal and after a quick shower and change, they walked down to the square. She suggested they eat at the small restaurant with the flower-bedecked terrace she had visited when she had first found the villa.

Surprisingly they seemed to remember her, although she was somewhat embarrassed when they assumed Mr Baker was her father.

However, he seemed highly amused and rather than explaining he was her boss, just told the waitress she was the daughter he had never had.

Once they had settled at a table for two on the terrace, he told her that as her 'adopted' father it wasn't right she still called him Mister, and from now on he was 'George.'

In the working London environment she would have found it difficult to change after all the years she had known him but somehow the more relaxed environment made it easier and she soon found herself naturally addressing him by his Christian name.

Although the new business was one topic of conversation, they soon moved on to more personal matters, comparing the differences and similarities of their new lives and how much had changed since they last worked together.

She found herself telling him about all the new friends she had made and he seemed delighted at the prospect of meeting Joseph the following morning.

When she admitted that she had surprised herself at the way she had changed and adapted, George replied that he had always known there was more to her than the efficient reserved secretary and overjoyed that from the chrysalis the beautiful butterfly had finally emerged.

Feeling totally relaxed in each other's company, she was not surprised when after paying the bill, he took her arm to escort her back to the villa.

After a final nightcap and his assurance that he had everything he needed, he bade her goodnight and after checking that the house was secure, she too went off to bed.

Chapter 34
People and parties

Waking early the next morning, Jane quickly showered and dressed then went down to start preparing breakfast for her guest.

Not long after, George appeared, looking fresh and rested, to wish her a cheery good morning as they sat together on the patio, still with the same comfortable relationship they had enjoyed the previous night.

They briefly discussed the future plans for the business, then Jane kept her promise and they walked down to the bookshop so she could introduce him to Joseph.

The two men hit it off immediately and after an hour or so she left them chatting while she went to prepare for this evening's party.

Stopping off at the various shops, she collected her orders and returned home to start getting things ready. She organised the area around the pool, made sure the wine was chilling and the cutlery and plates were all conveniently to hand, ready to set out on the tables later in the afternoon.

Things were going well when, about 1 o'clock, she heard a ring at the doorbell and for a moment her heart leaped, wondering if it could be Reno, only to be disappointed to find it was the bakers delivering her order as promised.

A short time later the bell rang again, only this time it was George apologising for being so long and hoping he hadn't put her out.

He had got on famously with Joseph and they had not noticed the time as they got carried away planning how their two businesses could work together for their mutual benefit.

When she offered to make lunch, George said he was a dab hand in the kitchen and the least he could do was take on that chore while she was busy.

True to his word, half an hour later, he called her to the patio where he had set out the pasta dish he had prepared, which she thoroughly enjoyed, especially as she hadn't had to cook it herself.

Afterwards he insisted on washing up, then came to help set out the tables and chairs ready for the evening.

By about 4 o'clock the beef was cooking slowly in the oven, the starters were keeping cool in the fridge and everything was under control.

After a refreshing cup of tea, George asked would she be offended if he took a quick nap, which seemed like a good idea with the long night ahead, so shortly afterwards she went to her own room to doze for an hour or so.

Waking sometime after five she went downstairs to find George had already started peeling the vegetables, so she left him to it while she went out to set the tables.

An hour later, with dusk falling, she turned on the fairy lights and couldn't help feeling satisfied at the overall effect their glow contributed to the ambience of the whole scene that met her eyes.

Going back upstairs, she bathed and dressed carefully and was gratified when George commented how beautiful she looked.

He too had changed and now looked very dapper and distinguished in dark trousers with a midnight-blue velvet jacket and cravat, very much the semi-formal English gentleman.

Deciding that deserved a toast, she opened one of the chilled bottles of wine and together they raised their glasses to the business and a happy and successful partnership.

Soon after she had checked that everything was ready and keeping warm in the kitchen, her guests began to arrive.

She was kept busy handing out drinks and making introductions. George was the perfect aide, taking on the role of barman, mingling with her guests and helping her carry out the starters when they sat down to eat about 8.30 ish.

By 10, when everyone had finished eating and complimented her on the delicious meal, he was adamant that she should stay with her guests while he cleared away and did the washing up.

With music playing and the background hum of contented conversation, Jane was pleased that everything had gone off so well, so when George returned she was happy to accept his invitation to join some of the others who were already dancing.

That seemed to be the signal for Frankie and some of the younger crowd to get her to join them in some of the more upbeat music, until laughing and pleading exhaustion, she collapsed into a chair for some liquid refreshment.

She hadn't heard the doorbell and assumed George must have let him in when about 11.30 she looked up to see Reno making his way towards her in between greeting the other guests, most of whom he already knew.

Once again she was not sure whether to be angry at his late arrival, or pleased that he had finally turned up.

Kissing her briefly on the cheek, she had no time to talk to him privately before they were joined by some of the others and they were involved in the general conversation. It was some time before the music changed to a slow romantic record and he took the opportunity to get her alone to dance.

Even then he didn't say much, just held her close and promised he would come by early the next evening if she was free.

As they went to sit down again, the party began to break up and Jane was involved in accepting thanks for a delightful evening and saying goodbye to her guests.

She was even more disappointed when the notary and his wife told her that Reno was giving them a lift home and, as they were standing waiting, he could only give her a quick, impersonal, kiss before they all left together.

By the time the last guest had left, George had cleared away the rest of the glasses and thanking her for a splendid time, said he was retiring to bed and would see her in the morning.

Thinking the rest could wait until tomorrow, she turned off the lights, checked the door and with a somewhat heavy heart went to her own bed to sleep alone.

Chapter 35
A day of surprises

Jane woke later than usual the next morning and when she came down, found that George had already stacked away the tables and chairs from the previous evening and was just preparing breakfast – the perfect houseguest.

While they were eating they discussed the party and the various people he had met.

At one stage he mentioned Reno and casually asked Jane if he was her 'young man.' Unsure how to respond, she merely said that they had been out together casually a few times but she had only known him a short while, so there was nothing serious between them.

Taking her hand George wished her the best of luck and said Reno would be mad to let her go as they were so perfectly suited.

Seeing her blush, George saved her any further embarrassment by pretending to flex his muscles and telling her that if Reno upset her, to let him know and he would come and sort him out.

The image of the small, elderly, wiry, man taking on the young, fit, hunk made her laugh, but such was his affection she actually believed he would do it.

After they had cleared up the breakfast dishes, George said he had promised to see Joseph again before he left and would she mind if he went over there for an hour or so.

Thinking that would give her a chance to go for a workout, she readily agreed and changing quickly, twenty minutes later they left the house together, parting at the square to go their separate ways and agreeing to meet later at Joseph's.

She worked hard at the gym and found it an excellent way of relieving some of her frustrations, so that when she left an hour and a half later she was much more relaxed and able to put things into perspective.

Arriving at the bookshop, she was taken aback for a moment to find the heavy wooden door closed, until she remembered it was Sunday.

Worried that George might be sitting outside the house waiting for her, she was just turning away to hurry home when the door suddenly opened and she was greeted by a plump, elderly, lady who smilingly invited her in.

Joking that it was no wonder Joseph was never home with a beautiful young lady like her helping him, she told Jane the 'boys' were still gossiping and led her through the shop to a small patio out the back where they were deep in conversation.

Breaking off as he saw her, George explained that Joseph and his wife had kindly invited him to lunch, if that was alright with her.

Saying that was fine and she would see him at home later, Jane was immediately told by Joseph's wife that the invitation obviously included her. No way was she leaving her to listen to these two old men, without some female company for a proper conversation.

Despite her protests that she had just come straight from the gym, Jane was given no option but to accept. She found herself seated with a glass of wine, while Joseph's wife put the finishing touches to lunch, chatting all the time to her while the men carried on their quiet conversation in the background.

She had to laugh when about half an hour later George and Joseph were instructed, as if they were two little boys, to stop talking and go and wash their hands as lunch was ready.

Meekly, but with a shared grin, both men did as they were told. They were soon all tucking into a delicious home-made soup, followed by roast chicken and salad, with a fruit laden trifle to finish off.

So much for the gym, thought Jane as they finished the meal. She felt so full she could hardly move.

A while later George reluctantly suggested they should be leaving soon and it was obvious to Jane that, in the short time they had known each other, the two men had become firm friends.

Returning home she had a quick shower and changed, while George packed up the rest of his things ready for his departure.

Although he had only been here a few days, she felt she had got to know him better than in all the years she had worked for him previously and realised she would actually miss him.

Soon they were at the airport and George told her that he would keep her informed about the launch party to be held in London. He made her promise she would be there, even assuring her that her flight costs and accommodation would be covered by the company.

After checking in and obtaining his boarding pass, they only had time for a quick coffee before the departure details for his own flight was announced. With a fatherly goodbye kiss and thanks for her hospitality, he went through security to the gate where his plane would be waiting to take him back to Spain.

Arriving safely home, once again the villa felt empty after her companionship of the weekend and the party of the night before.

It was now 4.30 and she wondered what Reno considered as early evening and if and when he would turn up.

No sooner had the thought crossed her mind than there was a ring at the door, which she opened to admit the man himself, who told her he had been sitting waiting in the car and seen her come back.

Still full of questions, she offered him a glass of wine and without waiting for an answer, set up the chilled bottle and glasses on the patio table.

Following her out, he pulled his chair closer to hers but for a while sat sipping his drink without saying anything.

To break the silence she told him that she had just returned from the airport after seeing her boss off and wasn't even sure whether he would turn up.

Leaning across the table to take her hand, he asked her if she really thought he was that shallow that he would break his promise.

Suddenly all the pent up frustration and anger came to the fore as she mockingly pointed out that he had disappeared without word for several days and only turned up at the last minute for her party, whereas she had wrongly assumed that he would be there to eat and spend the evening with her and her guests.

In answer to his explanation that he had been suddenly called away on business, with no chance to let her know, she sarcastically responded that she assumed that where he went they had no such things as telephones.

Without rising to her bait, he said yes, they did have telephones, but with the different time zones he didn't think she would appreciate being woken at 3 in the morning and wasn't his letter sufficient explanation.

Not having received any letter, she was still in two minds as to whether to believe him or not, but gradually his usual charm took over and when he kissed her properly, she forgot everything, including the fact that she was still angry with him.

One thing led to another and before she knew it they were in her bed and he was making love to her as if she was the most precious thing in the world to him.

All the emotions of the last few days and the passion of their reunion caught up with her and once again she found herself drifting off to sleep in the comfort of his arms.

Half asleep, she thought she caught the word darling, then waking fully, she heard him saying regretfully he had to go, but would contact her soon.

She watched him as he finished dressing, then blowing her a kiss from the bedroom door, once again he was gone.

She lay in bed for a while, her thoughts again in turmoil, then glancing at the clock, which showed it was just gone 8.30, decided she was hungry and got up to make herself something to eat.

Once she had finished her meal and cleared away, she tried to read a book for a while, but having read the same paragraph four or five times, gave up the effort and just let her thoughts take over.

Although when he was with her he was the perfect attentive lover, she couldn't help thinking how it was always Reno who had her at his beck and call, never making firm arrangements or letting her know where he was, or what he was doing.

While he seemed to enjoy their love making as much as she did, she was starting to feel used, as if he only contacted her when he wanted sex and then abandoned her until the next time he felt the urge, knowing she would be willing and available.

She was startled by the ringing of her phone and despite all her previous thoughts, her heart leaped, thinking it must be Reno phoning just to speak to her.

Realising it was a female voice, it took her a second or two to identify exactly who was babbling incoherently on the other end of the line.

"Jena, Calm down, I can't understand a word you're saying. What on earth's wrong?" Jane asked her sister when she was finally able to get a word in.

Fifteen minutes later she was still none the wiser, except that she had found herself promising to get the first available flight back to London and meet her sister at the apartment she had rented near to their old house.

What on earth was her sister doing back in England? Where was Mark? What had happened? These were all questions that would remain unanswered until she was able to talk to Jena face to face.

Chapter 36
Back to the airport

Having found it easier than she expected, Jane had confirmed her flight for 4 o'clock that afternoon to take her back to England to meet her sister and find out exactly what was going on.

She even had time to call into her neighbours, Gina and Raymond, to tell them she would be away for a few days and they readily agreed to keep an eye on the house. She then called in to see Joseph, who said he would miss her but they would catch up when she got back.

Unsure how long she would be away for and already thinking her wardrobe was more suited to a Mediterranean island than London streets, she packed a suitcase and already thought how she couldn't wait to get back 'home'.

Her thoughts turned to Reno but she had no way to contact him and part of her was even thinking, give as good as you get.

However she did phone the notary's office and left a message with Mr Borg's secretary that she would be away for a while, but upon her return would like an appointment to finalise arrangements for actually buying the property which she was currently renting.

As an afterthought she left her the temporary London address where she would be staying with her sister.

Having done everything she could to cover her absence, Jane resigned herself to being away from what she now counted as her proper life and booked a cab to take her to the airport for her afternoon flight.

It felt strange to be flying out to what used to be her home, whereas now the villa and her life here was what she thought of as home.

She was ready when the cab arrived and with a last glance back, already she missed her new life.

After checking in, she still had plenty of time and, with nothing better to do, spent an hour or so looking round the duty free and examining what the various shops had to offer.

The flight was uneventful and within a couple of hours she heard the announcement that they would soon be landing at Gatwick airport.

Looking out of the window at the dull grey skies, she was tempted to just turn around and take the next flight back but the thought of her sister waiting and needing her, made her face up to her responsibilities.

Clearing customs, she took a cab to the south London suburb, and within an hour was standing outside the address her sister had given her as her new home.

It was shortly after 8 o'clock when she rang the bell and her sister opened it to engulf her in a tearful bear hug to welcome her in.

With the emotion of the reunion and the practicalities of eating and sleeping arrangements, she had no chance to find out the reason behind the frantic phone call which had made her up sticks and return to London.

Retiring to the spare room and feeling like a stranger in a foreign land, she eventually managed to sleep to face what the following day would bring.

Chapter 37
London

Waking at her usual time the next morning, Jane found it strange not to find the sunlight streaming through the window until she remembered she was in the spare room with her sister back in London.

It was gone 11 before Jena finally emerged and Jane could start finding out what it was that had made her come flying back half way across the world.

Gradually the story emerged. The job Mark had been promised had failed to materialise, they had been living in a tiny rented flat where the air conditioning didn't work properly and she had suffered terribly from the heat.

With their money frittering away and no income, they had lost the dream house they had intended to buy and ended up doing nothing but arguing.

Being cooped up in the flat all day she had not got to know anyone and with no family or friends to talk to, had felt terribly homesick.

She couldn't even talk to Mark any more as he would come in frustrated and tired from job hunting and would just have something to eat and go off to bed, turning his back on her when she tried to get close to him.

She knew he felt guilty about not giving her the wonderful life he had promised but his refusal to even discuss it meant they were just drifting further and further apart.

Eventually she had just booked her flight and told him she was going home to London and what he did was up to him.

She had hoped he would follow her, but apart from a brief phone call had heard nothing from him.

Feeling she had no more tears to shed, she had put her name on various job sites and intended to start her life again near her childhood roots.

Over the next few days Jena's emotions see-sawed between bursting into tears at the slightest thing and over bright enthusiasm until Jane felt totally exhausted, not knowing from one minute to the next how her sister would react.

After some persuasion, she finally managed to convince her sister to see the doctor and, as she was still registered with their local GP, managed to make an appointment for a few days' time.

Although Jane had tried to do some work on her laptop, she found it difficult to concentrate and missed her usual 'office' environment of the patio by the pool and the warmth and friendship of her neighbours.

Most of all she missed Reno but, with no way of contacting him, she did feel a twisted pleasure that she had, albeit innocently, left him in the position of wondering where she was instead of the other way round.

One day drifted into another and Jane had started thinking about booking her flight home when she received an e-mail from George with details of the grand launch of his new business.

As it was only a few days away she decided to delay her return until after the event at the London hotel.

Jane had just returned from the supermarket, the day before the launch, when she was surprised to hear voices coming from the living room.

Calling hello and opening the door, she was greeted by the sight of Mark and Jena, cuddled up together on the settee, both with beaming smiles on their faces.

Mark explained that at first he had thought to stay on in Australia to prove himself but he had missed Jena so much that he had decided to swallow his pride and come back to the UK.

As soon as he had made his decision, he had contacted his old firm and they had been delighted to offer him a job in their new London office which was opening the following month.

There was even an explanation as to why Jena had been so emotional and unwell over the last few weeks, as the doctor had phoned to confirm that the results were positive – she was pregnant.

Both she and Mark were delighted, as although they had wanted a family, they had wondered if with her 40th birthday less than a year away, it might have made it more difficult for her to conceive.

With all that had happened, it wasn't until just before she was leaving for the launch party that Jena remembered the letter that had arrived for Jane the previous day. Opening it quickly after noticing the postmark, she found it was from the notary, but even after reading it twice still didn't believe the information it contained.

It seemed to be saying, in very formal legal language, that an offer had been received and accepted to buy the villa and asking for the details of her bank account to which her deposit should be refunded.

Completion would take place on the Saturday, in fact that very day and the handwritten note at the bottom said he would explain more when she returned.

Finding the notary's number in her mobile, she immediately tried to phone him but was disappointed, but not surprised, when a recorded voice told her the office was now closed and would re-open at 9 a.m. on Tuesday, after the bank holiday.

Realising it was already 6.30 p.m. here, which would be 7.30 on the island, there was nothing she could do except enjoy the party tonight and get in touch with him as soon as she could.

At that moment her cab arrived to take her into town and calling goodnight to Mark and Jena she set off for the hotel.

The warmth of the greeting when George saw her, helped to take her mind off her problems and she was impressed and delighted at the turnout of influential people who had come to wish him well.

Trying to keep track of all the names, she had to hide her embarrassment when George insisted on telling his guests that he couldn't have done it without her.

Even though it was not intended as an opportunity to drum up business, she found herself reaching for a notebook and pen to record various requests for further information and potential orders.

By midnight the success of the business was assured and as she took herself off to the room George had booked for her in the hotel for the night, she had a sense of achievement for a job well done.

At least things seemed to be going well in other people's lives; that just left her own to sort out.

Going down to breakfast the next morning, she had time to spend an hour with George to congratulate him on his success before he left for the airport to catch an early flight back to his home in Spain.

That made her think of going home too and she determined that as soon as she got back she would look up flight times to take her back to the island.

With Jena happy and back with Mark, there was nothing to keep her in London and even if she no longer had her perfect home there, she was determined to find another place to live so she could stay on the island.

Thinking about it, she couldn't help but feel betrayed by Mr and Mrs Molina who, after all their promises, had gone over her head to accept another offer.

Although she couldn't blame them, as the price she had offered was ridiculously low for such a superb property, she did feel that they had let her down by at least not discussing it with her first.

There again, maybe they had tried to contact her, but as she was out of the country they might have been compelled to move fast.

What was done was done, she decided eventually and it was no use worrying about it now.

Arranging with reception to call her a cab, she was soon on her way back to her temporary London home.

Getting back to the rented property about midday on Sunday, she felt like the proverbial spare part as Mark and Jena acted like honeymooners, which reinforced her decision to book her flight as soon as possible.

Unfortunately, fate seemed to have conspired against her, as a strike by air traffic controllers in France, coupled with school holidays, meant the first available flight was not until late on Tuesday evening.

She spent most of Monday working on her computer, following up the leads from the launch party and trying to keep out of the way of Mark and Jena, who were house hunting in London in preparation for nest building for their forthcoming family.

They returned, glowing with excitement, late Monday afternoon, unable to believe their luck at the turn of fate which had given them first option on the perfect property.

Although happy for them, Jane couldn't help comparing their housing news with her own and it was only after lots of hints and directives to guess where it was, that she gave in and asked them outright the location of the property.

It turned out that the purchasers of their old family home had unexpectedly had to go to the north of England, where their employers had relocated and the house had come back on the market.

Wanting a quick sale, they had been delighted to accept the proposed offer, at slightly less than the original sale price. Jena and Mark would be moving back into the house where the girls had been brought up.

It would also mean that the furniture Jane had put into storage could be retrieved, which she supposed was one less thing to worry about.

Phoning the notary first thing Tuesday morning Jane was informed that he was out at meetings all day and had to be contented with an appointment for Thursday morning.

With nothing to occupy her time until her flight, Jane couldn't help reflecting on how the changes in her life had come full circle.

Here she was, back in London with her sister who was moving back into the house they had shared with their parents, while Jane was no longer sure if she had a home to call her own.

Even her blonde highlights had grown out, so that her hair was returning to its original light brown and in need of a cut. Her clothes were sensible English autumn, rather than the frivolous Mediterranean summer wear she had become accustomed to.

Her liaison with Reno seemed like a dream and even if she saw him again, she had no idea whether he was looking at their relationship as a brief fling which was nice while it lasted.

For a while she toyed with the idea of cancelling her flight and just reverting to her old life in London.

At least she would have a home, as there was plenty of space in the old house and she could even have her old bedroom back.

The thought didn't last for long as, despite the familiarity of her old life, she knew now she was no longer the same person and her heart belonged on the island.

Decision made, she packed her suitcase, checked her passport and booked a cab to take her back to whatever the future might hold for her.

Chapter 38
The end and the beginning

Jane slowly opened her eyes and lay thinking about the events of the last three months.

She couldn't believe how much her life had changed again.

The feel of her husband's arm stretching out to rest on her stomach made her smile as if he was reassuring himself that their baby was safe and happy.

Jena's baby would have a cousin only a few months younger to visit and get to know as he grew up, or even two, as the doctor had said it was highly likely she was having twins.

They would also be growing up in the house of her dreams, as Reno had been the mysterious purchaser who had bought the villa as an engagement present for her. She had finally forgiven him for the sleepless nights she had spent until she saw the notary who had explained everything.

She smiled as she remembered his surprise when she reminded him that he had omitted to tell her that he wanted to marry her, until she had seen him waiting for her when she returned to the island.

Subconsciously she had always realised that he was more than a handyman employed by the hotel group, so it was not a total surprise when he explained that following his father's retirement he was now the Managing Director of the whole corporation, which was the reason for his sudden and unexplained absences.

Although he had promised her that when the children were old enough he would take her to visit every hotel in the chain, for the time being it was enough that apart from short trips abroad, he would be here with her every day to love and to cherish, for ever and ever. Amen